I0638729

RETURN TO VEGAS

ELENA AITKEN

INKBLOT COMMUNICATIONS

ISBN: 978-1-927968-40-6

This is a work of fiction. The events and characters described herein are imaginary and are not intended to refer to specific places or living persons. The opinions expressed in this manuscript are solely the opinions of the author and do not represent the opinions or thoughts of the publisher. The author has represented and warranted full ownership and/or legal right to publish all the materials in this book.

This book is dedicated to every single one of my readers. Always believe in love.

CHAPTER ONE

~Lexi~

The clock over the door ticked its steady rhythm, and I took one more look around the room. Time was almost up. Most of the kids were already done with their test and had their heads down on the desk the way I'd instructed them to do when they finished. There were a few who still hastily scribbled away on their papers, and when the bell rang, I expected to see their crestfallen expressions, but it still didn't make it any easier. I had a handful of kids who tried so hard, but despite all their hard work and all the extra time I put in with them, grade four math just wasn't clicking. They weren't going to be happy with their marks. Neither would their parents. The kids took off as soon as the bell rang and I gave them permission to clear out. All except one. I waited a beat before I got up to collect the papers. He sat at the back of the room, staring intently at his paper as if he could change the answers he'd recorded by sheer will. I purposely took my time working my way through the room, giving him all the time I could.

Finally, I couldn't put it off any longer. "You did good, Conner." I took his paper and offered him a smile, because it was all I could give him.

"Thanks, Ms. Titan. But if I don't pass grade four, my dad will kill me and—"

"I have no doubt you'll pass, Conner. You've been working really hard." And it was true. Conner was a good kid with a huge heart. It hadn't all clicked for him academically yet, but it would. I had no doubt. He reminded me of Ben at that age. Smart kid, just needed the right motivator. We were getting there. At least with Conner. Ben seemed to be a different story these days. "Now stop worrying about it. You did all you could. Go enjoy your afternoon, okay?"

I knew the second he left the room he'd stop worrying about fractions and start concentrating on whether the ice on the lake was frozen thick enough yet. It seemed to be the prime worry for all the little boys in town—and most of the big ones too.

But not Leo.

My heart both skipped a beat and stopped for a split second. A mixed feeling, to be sure. Because although after five years of waking up in his arms, turning to look into those deep brown eyes, he still made me feel like a teenager in love, it was the twinge of fear that caused me to pause that was new. Well, if I was honest, it'd been there for a while, slowly building. When the seasons changed again, the air grew cold and the snow began to fly, the fear and worry were all I could think about when it came to Leo.

Last winter hadn't been easy. I'd lived through some impressive Canadian winters in my life, but maybe I'd managed to block out the worst of them, because when the never ending storms came, snowing us into the cabin more than once, even I suffered through the endless cold and long, dark nights. Summer had been too short, as summers always were. But with every day that passed, I watched Leo, and I could see the worry lines around his eyes creasing. And I knew exactly what caused them. The winter winds not only kept business away from the inn, but they kept my active, warm-weather loving husband shuttered indoors. Like a caged animal, he'd spend the next few months pacing the floor, trying to find something to keep him busy when there was nothing he could do that would compare to simply going outside without a parka on.

He hadn't said anything, at least not to me, but I knew it was weighing on him. If we had another bitter cold season, it wasn't just the inn that would suffer.

I stuffed my papers into my bag and gathered the last few things I'd need for the evening. I tried to hurry because Ben was supposed to be waiting for me at the front doors. At almost twelve, he wanted so badly to have his freedom and walk home from school with the other boys; at least, that's what he said around them. Secretly, I think he liked those quiet moments we spent together. It was a few minutes of quiet, just the two of us. At least that's what I liked to believe and I was hanging onto it.

Not quite a teenager but no longer a boy, Ben constantly struggled for independence and with the insecurity that came with the awkward pre-teen years. It was a continuing battle and one that only escalated as his hormones started to kick in. Almost a teenager. *God.* The thought continually hit me out of the blue. My baby was going to be a teenager in only a few short years. The age gap between Ben and any future siblings was only getting wider. Not that I wanted it that way. In fact, quite the opposite. My hand instinctively went to my stomach the way it'd been doing more and more for the last few weeks.

Maybe this one would stick?

It was a terrible way to think, but I couldn't help it. Three miscarriages had taken their toll and I refused to get my hopes up with either the pregnancy or what I hoped beyond hope would be the outcome. It was too painful. Besides, there was nothing to even think about until I took a test and knew either way what I was dealing with. I should have taken the test weeks ago. Maybe even months ago, but my body was less than reliable these days and missing a period wasn't all that unusual. Besides, secretly I thought that maybe if I ignored it, it would hurt less when the inevitable happened. Again.

By the time I'd fed the class hamster and flicked the lights out, I was running a few minutes late and Ben wasn't in the hall where he was supposed to meet me.

"Perfect." I scanned the hall. No Ben.

It was happening more and more. He was using any excuse to take off and leave with his friends. Maybe I was wrong, and he didn't cherish those quiet moments quite as much as I thought he did. The thought sparked a twinge of pain in my chest. Leo kept telling me I was deluding myself with the fact that Ben was growing up. I wanted to keep him little for a bit longer. It was a losing battle, and I knew it. But it didn't stop me from trying.

"Are you talking to yourself again?" Liz Walker, who taught the one grade-six class in our small school, came up beside me and nudged me with her elbow. "You know it's a sign of insanity, right?"

"If you had a pre-teen boy, you'd be going insane, too."

She threw her head back and laughed. It was a sound that never failed to cheer me up. It was almost impossible to be grouchy or sad when you were surrounded by someone as vivacious as Liz. "I'm surrounded by twelve of them every day, Lex. And just as many pre-teen girls, which is arguably worse. Much worse."

I shook my head because she had a point.

"But I feel for you," Liz added. "I really do. It can't be easy. But Ben's a good kid. He'll be okay. Come on, I'll walk out with you."

It was a handy thing to be friends with Ben's teacher, because in the next five minutes, I got an update about his schoolwork, including the assignment he hadn't handed in. I was fairly positive that Ben wouldn't agree with me about the convenience of his mother being buddies with his teacher, but it did have its perks.

"I'll talk to Ben about the story," I promised Liz as we walked out into the chilly afternoon air. As cool as it was, it wasn't cold enough to freeze the lake fully. Not yet anyway. It was only mid-November. There was lots of time for the cold to settle in.

Lots of time.

I may not have thought it was very cold, but I had no doubt that Leo was bundled up and next to the fire at the inn, worrying about the cold and money and bookings and pretty much everything that was out of his control. And a number of things that were in his control. But he'd worry anyway, because that seemed to be more and more what he did lately. He'd been way too stressed out lately, and not for the first time I wished I could give him a reprieve from the stress. Even for a little while.

My hand went to my stomach again and I bit my lip.

I looked down the street in the direction where Ben would have gone with his buddies. It was a long walk home, considering we lived out of town, in the area that was thought primarily of as the renters' cottages. And it was, too, but that's why I liked it so much. It was quiet. With no real neighbors for most of the year, it was almost as if we lived all on our own. Besides that, it had been Uncle Ray's special place for years, and I'd never sell it.

Never.

After Uncle Ray died, the cabin was the only real connection Ben and I had to him.

Of course, the house hadn't been designed to be lived in year round—well, it hadn't really been designed to be lived in at all. It had been built as a cabin, a summer retreat.

The insulation was just another concern that Leo was probably worrying about. We'd talked about replacing the windows before the snow flew and getting some better insulation sprayed into the walls to help keep the house warm and cut down on our heating bill. I'd been tucking away money for the last few years, and then there was our savings, a small inheritance that Uncle Ray had left us. But I didn't want to touch it. Either way, I knew we had enough by now but I hated to bring it up, because although he'd never say anything, I knew Leo didn't want to put more money into winterizing the house. I think secretly he hoped I would wake up one morning and decide it was too cold in the Canadian Rockies and we should move.

Not that the thought hadn't crossed my mind. Because it had. Sure, I loved the lake. There were a lot of memories here. It was Uncle Ray's house, but that was the problem, too. It was Uncle Ray's house. We'd lived in the cottage for almost five years, but despite spending all that time there, it still didn't seem like our place yet. To be fair, I probably hadn't tried hard enough. The years had been busy. Leo spent all his time at the Lake Lillian Inn, transforming it into a thriving business and for me, building up a whole curriculum for grade four from scratch took time. Let alone getting Ben adjusted to his entirely flipped upside-down life. He'd adjusted much better than I'd expected to finding out his *father* wasn't really his father and Leo, a man he'd just met, was his father and we were in love and moving to the lake. It was a lot for anyone, let alone a little boy. But he was resilient and not only had he adjusted, he'd thrived.

Despite that, we still hadn't settled in and the problem was I'd been using the same excuses for years and that's all they were.

Excuses.

~Leo~

GOD, she was beautiful.

Always.

Even bundled up in that thick black coat of hers that I hated so much, she looked amazing as she walked through the doors of the Lake Lillian Inn. I flipped my laptop shut, tossed it to the couch next to me and left the warmth of the fire where I'd been working on some new marketing ideas to greet the love of my life properly.

I pulled her close and swallowed whatever it was she was going to say with a kiss. But I could never only have a taste of Lexi. It was never enough. With one hand keeping her close, I unbuttoned just enough of that dammed coat to slip a hand inside and onto her sexy curves. She moaned. Just a little, and only so I could hear, but it was all the encouragement I needed. There wasn't much I could do about it in the foyer of the inn, but when we got home...

My hand slipped around to run down the swell of her breasts and rest on her stomach, just over the line of her belt. And just like that, the kiss was over. Lexi pulled away, that look on her face. The look I couldn't stand because it reminded me just how much she was hurting. I should have known better. Ever since the last miscarriage, she would barely let me look at her stomach, let alone touch it.

"Lex, I'm—"

"It's fine." She straightened her hair and tightened her coat around her. There was a smile on her face, but it was tight and forced. Not the smile I wanted to see. "I'm sorry to bother you, but..." She glanced around, likely to see whether anyone was there to overhear us, but it was November, one of the slowest months at the inn, despite every effort I'd made with marketing. Bump season, the time between the summer and winter seasons, was one of the hardest challenges I'd ever had to overcome managing a hotel. Of course, there was no bump season in Vegas. A lot of things were different in the Canadian Rockies. Including my family.

"You're not bothering me." I took her hand and led her to the couches in front of the fire where I'd been working. "You know I love it when you visit. How was school? Where's Ben?"

Her face shifted again, and instead of sitting, she popped back up and paced. "I was hoping he'd be here."

"Here?"

"He didn't wait for me again, and I assumed he'd be at home after walking with his buddies. But he's not and well, I was hoping he'd be here with you."

I could count on one hand how many times Ben had come to the inn on his own to hang out with me in the last year. He used to ride his bike down the gravel roads to spend time with me whenever he could. I'd had him painting, cleaning, hauling boxes, you name it. Ben loved helping out. Or at least, he had. Now that he was in grade six, things were different. But it was perfectly normal. Or at least that's what Lexi told me. I really had no idea. "He's not here." I shrugged. Lexi got a lot more worked up about these things than I did. It was a small town, and Ben was a kid. He'd be fine; it was all part of growing up. Hell, when I was his age, I was by myself most of the time. I definitely didn't have a mom hovering over me, worrying about where I was every second of the day. Ben was old enough to hang out with his friends. In fact, I encouraged it. Not that I was about to suggest that to Lexi.

At least not at the moment. I was smarter than that. There was definitely a time and a place to mention things like that. And it wasn't right then.

"I'm sure he's fine, Lex. He probably just forgot to tell you he was going to Marcus's house. You know boys, they're pretty forgetful and—"

"He should have told me." Lexi spun around again. "He knows I worry and I think it's more than that. Something's going on."

"What do you mean?"

She turned to look at me. Her hair flipped over her shoulder; the sight distracted me for a moment, but only a moment. "I talked to Liz today," she said. "She was telling me Ben didn't hand in a short story assignment. That's not like him at all," Lexi continued. "Ben doesn't blow off homework. He just doesn't."

"He's a pre-teen boy."

"That's not an excuse."

"No. But it's the reality."

Lexi shook her head and turned away to look out the window. "No. It's not our reality. I refuse to allow Ben to flunk grade six."

I went up behind her and rubbed my hands up and down her arms. She still hadn't taken off that jacket, and I had to fight to keep from doing it for her, but there'd be time for that later. For the moment, calming her down was way more important. When Lexi got worked up, she could really get herself going. And I knew Ben was fine. Of course he was. "He's not going to flunk grade six. He's a smart kid."

"Is he?" She spun in my arms and I caught her tight. "Is he really? Do smart kids blow off assignments? No. It's not like him, Leo. It's not like him at all."

I couldn't disagree with that. It wasn't like Ben to ignore homework. He was a good kid who got good grades. Something was definitely up with him. I just didn't know what. But I would. After dinner, I'd take Ben for a walk with the dog and we'd get to the bottom of things. I told Lexi as much.

"That's good, Leo. It is, but..."

"But?"

There was more going on with her. Something she wasn't saying. And for a moment, I thought she was going to tell me, but then her mouth closed and her lips pressed into a line, the way it was more and more these days. "No but."

Her smile was sweet and even though I didn't believe her for a second, I smiled and pulled her close to press a kiss to her forehead. "Okay, babe. Are you headed home? Or do you want to stick around?"

She shook her head and rebuttoned her coat. "No, I should get going. I have tests to grade and I need to stop at the store and..."

"And? What do you need? If you have work to do, I can stop for you. Just give me a list."

Her face transformed into a beautiful smile that lit up her whole face. I knew just how much it meant to her when I offered to run the simple errands for her. It was no big deal for me, but for her...well, if I could do anything to put that smile on her face, I would. Every time.

"Just a few things," she started. "Milk, some fruit, and—you know what?" The smile fell from her face and she shook her head hard. "I'll go."

"Seriously, it's no bother. I wanted to talk to Seth about taking on some more hours, anyway. It's no trouble." Seth and his wife, Enid, ran the general store, but after convincing Seth to quit teaching and come work for me at the inn last year, he had been taking on more and more jobs for me, and I know he had real potential to manage things in my absence. Not that I had an absence planned or anything, but a holiday would definitely be a good idea and I was determined that this would be the year that Lexi and I got away. Maybe we could even take Ben to Vegas and show him where we met....

"I got it, Leo."

I returned my attention to Lexi in time to see her turn and head for the front door. "I'll just pop in and meet you at home, okay?"

"If you're sure."

"Of course."

I bit my tongue because there was absolutely no point in pushing her if she didn't want to be pushed. Instead, I grabbed her arm and pulled her into me to give her a kiss that left nothing to the imagination. "I look forward to seeing you later," I whispered in her ear before I sucked her lobe into my mouth the way I knew would send a thrill through her entire body.

She gave me a sexy smile that promised of more later, but when she finally turned and slipped out the front door, I couldn't help but shake the feeling that not only was our son going through something I was going to have to figure out, but so was his mother.

CHAPTER TWO

~Lexi~

Leo knew me better than anyone, and I could see it in his eyes that he was worried about me. But he'd be even more worried if I'd asked him to pick up the pregnancy test. I couldn't put that stress on him right now. Not when I could see how he was struggling already.

No. He didn't need to know. Not until there was something to know.

Fortunately for me, Enid Lawson, one of my closest friends, and the owner of the general store, didn't even raise an eyebrow when she scanned my purchases. She knew my struggle, and she knew me well enough to know that if I wanted to talk about it, I would.

Enid and I have been friends for years, and besides Nicole, she was definitely my best friend, maybe even more so because I saw her more these days because Nicole and Ryan lived in the city. We saw them quite a bit when they were first married and

Leo moved up to Canada. But...life happens, people got busy and now that they were expecting their first child, it was even harder. More than hard. I wanted nothing more than to give Leo another child and Ben a brother or sister. I did my best to be a supportive best friend and listen to all of Nicole's experiences, but I'd be lying if I said it hadn't stung a little every time she texted me a picture of her growing belly.

But more and more, it didn't look like it was going to happen. Except...I sat in the car outside the house and clutched the box that held the stick that would tell my future. I turned it around in my hands and clutched it to my chest briefly before stuffing it into my purse. I grabbed up the rest of the bags and made my way up to the house. If Ben wasn't in his room working on his homework, there'd be hell to pay.

Leo was always telling me to relax a little and give him some more space, but as a mother, that was almost impossible to do. Besides, I was trying. I really was. I'm not stupid, and I remember well what it was like to be a pre-teen and then, even worse, a teenager.

No. I knew the key to parenting was to give him just enough support to let him know I was there for him no matter what. And trust. Sure, he'd make mistakes, but I needed to trust him.

I took a deep breath before I went inside. It was hard, but I would try.

The second I saw Ben's running shoes in a pile beside the closet—instead of in it—I exhaled hard. He was home.

Skip, Ben's dog, ran over to greet me, happily licking my hand as I tried to pet him.

"He's home, is he, Skip?"

The dog looked at me, barked once and took off running. No doubt to warn Ben I was home. "Traitor," I called after him. "Remember who buys your food." There was nothing to do but shake my head and deposit my groceries in the kitchen. Skip really was a good dog. A very early gift to Ben from Leo and named after skipping rocks. A skill Uncle Ray had tried to teach Ben right before he passed. He was definitely a special dog. In so many ways. And he was very loyal to Ben, a detail that made me both shake my head and smile.

A few minutes later, Ben wandered into the kitchen, his head down and looking at his feet that he shuffled along the hardwood in the way that made me crazy. "Hey, Mom."

"Ben." I tried to play it cool. I had to. If I got mad right away, he'd get defensive and any chance I might have of talking to him about whatever was really going on with him would be gone. No. I needed to try a softer approach. "I missed you after school. Did you walk home with your friends?"

"Nah." He shuffled to the fridge and grabbed the jug of orange juice.

"You walked by yourself?" It wasn't the answer I expected and I tried not to let him see that it took me off guard. "Maybe tomorrow we can walk together? I'll leave the car at home and—"

"Maybe." He poured himself a big glass of juice, and I tried to bite my tongue.

"Juice is for breakfast, buddy. We're going to have dinner soon. Your father should be—" I stopped talking when I noticed his face. "Ben? What's going on? Are you okay?"

He nodded but wouldn't look at me.

"You know, if you want to talk about it..."

For a second, I didn't think he'd say anything, but then a single tear rolled down his cheek. He swiped it away quickly, but I'd already seen it. I smiled as encouragingly as I could and that's all it took for him to talk. "All the kids hate me."

His words took the air from my lungs. I fought to maintain composure. "What are you talking about?" I pulled the carton of milk from the shopping bag and did my best to look casual as I put the groceries away, but all I really wanted to do was wrap my arms around my little boy, hug him tight and protect him from the hurts of the world. "That can't be true."

"It is. They make fun of me and steal my lunches."

"Your lunches?"

Ben nodded and sank onto the barstool across from me.

"What do you mean, they make fun of you?" I dreaded the answer, but I had to know. I couldn't not ask.

He dropped his head to the countertop and mumbled something into his arms.

"What was that?"

Ben looked up; tears streamed down his face. "They call me a bastard."

"They call you a what?" I almost dropped the jar of pickles I was holding, but managed to put it down on the counter before I caused a terrible mess. "Why would they call you such a thing? Your friends? Who calls you that? Boys your age shouldn't even know that word."

"Mom. We all know that word."

"What do you think it means?" I prayed he didn't know the answer.

"It means you're not married to Dad."

Dammit.

I racked my brain to think of something I could say that wouldn't be a lie, but would also make everything okay. I came up empty. But empty wasn't an option. "You know that's not true, right, Ben?"

His face lit up but was also lined with confusion. "You *are* married to Dad?"

"Well, no." I shook my head and nodded at the same time. "I mean, yes. That's true. I'm not married to your dad. Yet." It was a *yet* I wasn't entirely comfortable giving considering Leo and I had talked about marriage off and on for years and never managed to commit to anything. Which was ridiculous, because we couldn't be more committed to each other. Years ago, we had a wedding date set, but then the first miscarriage happened and we canceled everything. After that, it didn't seem like something we needed to do. Clearly, we'd both made an error in judgment. Even if we didn't think it was necessary to have a ceremony to declare our love for each other, Ben obviously did. I took a deep breath and exhaled slowly. "Just because we're not married doesn't mean we're any less of a family. You know that, right, buddy?"

He nodded, but I wasn't fooled.

"It's not that we don't want to get married."

"Who doesn't want to get married?"

Leo chose that moment to walk in the door. He headed directly over to me, where he dropped a kiss on the top of my head before he ruffled Ben's hair in the way that we all knew he hated these days, but only tolerated from his dad. He had perfect timing and I could have cried from the relief of having backup for this particular conversation.

"Mom was just trying to tell me why you weren't married yet."

Leo's handsome face twisted into a sly smile and he twisted his head around to look at me. *Shit.* He was clearly not going to be the backup I was looking for.

"Is that right?" he said slowly. "And what has your mom given as an explanation?"

I muttered a string of words under my breath and shot Leo a look that he would have no trouble deciphering.

"She didn't." With his father around, Ben's entire presence changed. He stood taller, his shoulders pulled back, full of confidence. "All she said was that it didn't mean you didn't love each other."

"Well, that's true." Leo winked at me, knowing how it

melted me. "But it does mean we've been really busy for the last few years, and we haven't had much time to think about planning something."

Was that the reason? I'd long ago stopped asking Leo about it. With my parents and Uncle Ray gone, the idea of a big wedding didn't really appeal to me, and if Leo didn't care...well, it never seemed to matter much. We both knew how much we loved each other, he'd been able to secure a work visa for Canada, and we were happy. There didn't really seem to be a reason to go to the trouble. Except...I looked at Ben's face, so full of hope and question. Apparently there was a reason we'd never stopped to consider.

"You know what, Ben?" I took his hand in mine and to my surprise, he didn't pull away as he did more often than not lately. "I think maybe it's time we made the time to plan a wedding. What do you think?"

He smiled like the little boy he still was and nodded with enthusiasm. "Yes. Because then I can be the ring bearer and when Marcus was a ring bearer in his cousin's wedding a few years ago, he got a present."

I shook my head. He was nothing if not predictable.

Leo laughed. "Sounds good, but you can't be the ring bearer."

"What?"

"Why not?"

Ben and I asked at the same time.

Leo wrapped one arm around me and tugged our son close. "Because you, my son, will be the best man."

~Leo~

By the time Lexi and I were done talking to Ben about his troubles at school, I still wasn't totally convinced that getting married would solve all his problems. In fact, I knew it wouldn't. But it would be a good thing for all of us, and maybe it would even help Lexi out of whatever funk she'd been in for the last little bit. I knew the miscarriages had been hard on her. Hell, they'd been hard on both of us, but there was no way I could understand how she'd felt losing the pregnancies. That much I knew.

I watched her from across the bedroom as she carefully folded her sweater and tucked it away in the closet. God, she was beautiful. The last few years and everything her body had gone through hadn't changed a thing. At least not in my eyes. I knew Lexi thought differently, which was why she instinctively turned away from me before she took her t-shirt off and pulled her pajama top over her head.

Damn. It had been way too long since I'd had my hands on her skin. Little over a month. Not that I was counting, but I remembered the night well. Ben had a sleepover with his buddy, so I'd made a romantic dinner, brought home a bottle of wine, which she didn't partake in—she never did anymore—and we'd sat on the deck talking, wrapped under thick blankets on one of those rare warm fall nights. It had been a great night together time, followed by an even better time between the sheets.

A low growl rumbled in my throat. God, I missed her. And I'd be damned if I wasn't going to do anything about it. I dropped the book I was holding onto the bedside table and crossed the room in two long strides. She jumped a little when my arms wrapped around her waist, but I pulled her close so she was pressed up the length of me. My body responded instantly to her shape. The heat of her penetrated the thin cotton of the pajamas I wore.

"Leo. What are you—"

I quieted her questions with my lips on her neck. Her hair was soft in my hand as I stroked it and pulled it to the side to give me better access to the silky skin on her neck. Her body shook gently when I moved my kisses around to her earlobe. I knew exactly how sensitive her neck was, and even though it had been awhile, her body responded readily when I sucked her lobe gently into my mouth, swirling my tongue all around her ear, tracing the edges before darting in, just enough to make her moan.

I pulled away and whispered, "I think you know exactly what I'm doing."

The sigh that escaped her lips was all the encouragement I needed to slide my hands down her sides, tracing the swell of her breasts with my hands as I moved down. I skipped quickly over her abdomen; my hands rested on her hips before I pulled her even tighter against me. The woman had never failed to drive me completely wild.

"Leo, I—"

The last thing I needed to hear was any kind of objection or excuse, so I spun her around in my arms and kissed her sweet mouth until she melted into me.

~Lexi~

I COULD THINK of a million reasons why I shouldn't have sex. Not the least of which was an unused pregnancy test still tucked into my purse. But with Leo's mouth on mine, sparking feelings in me that only he could bring out, all rational thought went out the window. All I could think about was how it had been too long since we'd been intimate without the pressure of making a baby. I almost told him about the test in my purse, but when he kissed me as if he needed me to breathe, I pushed it out of my head and focused only on the man in front of me. The way it should be.

He lifted me easily as if I weighed nothing and instead of protesting, I wrapped my legs around him and let him back me up against the wall. My hands slid across his bare chest, still as chiseled and hard as it was when we'd met, only now the muscles were more defined from years of living in the mountains: chopping wood, shoveling snow, and all the rest of the physical labor that came with it. He'd never looked sexier, which is why it was so crazy that we weren't intimate more often. Was it me? Was it—

"Lexi." His voice interrupted my train of thought and I turned to look into his dark eyes. "Stop thinking so much." He kissed me hard. His hand cupped my face and held me firmly in place before he pulled away. "Just let go, babe."

So I did.

I wrapped my arms around him, and returned his kiss with a ferocity I hadn't let myself feel in far too long. Leo was right. I thought about everything way too much when all I really needed to do was stop thinking and just enjoy the moment and the man I loved.

He groaned in appreciation and I could feel his desire grow even harder against me. "That's what I'm talking about." He turned and carried me effortlessly to our bed, where he placed me before he grabbed the hem of my pajama shirt and tugged it over my head. Reflexively, I moved to cover my chest, but the look in his eyes stopped me.

Despite the changes my body had been through, this man still thought I was the sexiest woman alive, and in that moment I knew it was true. At least for him. And that's all that mattered.

I raised my arms up and lifted my hair off my back in a slow move, never letting my gaze leave his. I could see the desire darken in his eyes as he took in my body from my neck down to my exposed breasts. My nipples pebbled under his intense scrutiny and that's when I let my hair fall, cascading over my shoulders before I reached forward and tugged his pajama pants down over his hips. My hands lingered on the tight muscles of his behind. They flexed under my fingers so I dug in, just a little.

Leo made a sound halfway between a groan and a growl and moments later had kicked his pants to the side and hovered over me, a look of pure primal need on his face. It sent shivers through me and when he dropped his mouth to kiss me again, I was all but lost to him and the desire he stirred in me.

"I need you."

"Babe, I need you so bad." Leo tugged my panties off, throwing them somewhere behind him, and in the next instant was inside me. Almost cautiously at first and as he filled me, I sighed in deep satisfaction. Any tentativeness was gone as he drove home his need for me.

After, as Leo pulled me close so my back was pressed against him, he stroked my arm. His fingers traveled the length of me and a contentment filled me until it threatened to overwhelm me. A tear slipped from my eye and down my cheek. I dared not move to wipe it away, but Leo noticed anyway.

"Lex? Are you okay?"

I nodded but didn't trust myself to speak. The rush of emotion was unexpected and way too much.

"Lexi?" He slipped his arm out from under me and sat up, rolling me to look up at him before I could bury my face. "What's going on? Did I hurt you?" It killed me to see how his eyes flew immediately to my stomach. *How had it happened that we'd gotten to this point?*

I shook my head quickly. "No. I'm fine. You didn't...I'm fine."

Confusion clouded his eyes, but I didn't know how to explain what I was feeling when I didn't even know myself.

"Honestly, Leo." I tried to force a laugh but it came out more like a strange choke. "I'm fine. I don't know what that was all about. I mean." I reached for him and pulled him back down to lie next to me. "That was amazing." I stroked his back, letting my fingers trace patterns on his skin. "We should do that more often."

That made the corners of his mouth turn up into a smile. "Yes, we most definitely should. And I think now is a good start."

I laughed as he kissed down my arm, sending tickles through my body while at the same time his hands slid up my thighs.

"Okay, okay." I swatted his hand away, because as much as I would like a repeat of what we'd just enjoyed, I also needed some sleep if I was going to be of any use to my class tomorrow. Because I'd been so busy talking with Ben about his problems in class, I hadn't gotten around to grading the students' papers, so I'd need to set my alarm to get up early and complete the grading.

And take a test of your own, a voice in the back of my head reminded me.

The pregnancy test still sat, wrapped tightly in its packaging, in my purse. And yes, I would take that test in the morning, too. But at that moment, with Leo holding me tight, loving me not only despite my flaws, but because of them, the pressure I'd felt about it earlier was gone. No matter what the test said, it wouldn't matter because I had everything I already needed.

~Leo~

THERE WAS nothing better than Lexi drifting off to sleep in my arms. Her content little sighs escaping her lips like puffs of air on my arm made me smile and I pulled her closer to drop a kiss on the top of her head. There wasn't a day that went by that I didn't thank the heavens above for the life I had with Lexi and Ben. Fate brought us together all those years ago when we fell in love on the streets of Las Vegas, and I didn't care what anyone said, it was fate that brought us together again all those years later: Her with a five-year-old son—my son. Me with only the memory of the girl who'd meant everything and slipped away.

I was a lucky man. Of that there was no doubt and despite the fact that we'd tried without success to expand our family, it didn't matter. We were perfect, just the three of us.

At the lake.

In the mountains.

In a small town.

A *very* small town.

Stop it. I needed to force those thoughts out of my head. They were coming far too frequently these days. It wasn't that I didn't love my life. I did. But I'd be lying if I said I didn't miss the excitement of the big city and the challenge of running a large resort hotel.

And I was lying. Every single day. But if my choice was a big city hotel or my family, it was no contest. I snuggled Lexi even closer to me. No. There was no choice to make.

The Lake Lillian Inn had been a huge success and a huge challenge. It was falling into almost complete disrepair when I'd bought it. A struggling little hotel with no prospects and no future. But I'd changed that. In a big way. Now it was thriving. As much as it could, anyway. We offered company retreats, weddings, even ladies' weekends that included scrapbooking. I still shook my head at that one. When Lexi suggested it, I had no idea what to expect, but what I didn't envision was a dozen women with crafting supplies and endless bottles of wine to descend on my little hotel. As it turned out, it was one of the more profitable ideas we'd had, and the inn now offered them quarterly. The retreats had a preferred placement on the schedule.

The schedule.

That was part of the problem. The inn more or less ran itself. The challenge was gone. I craved a challenge. Something to really sink my teeth into. The idea of what that challenge might be had kept me up on more than one occasion. As the hours ticked by, and my arm fell asleep under Lexi, I realized I was in for another night of sleeplessness. Finally, I slid my tingling arm out from under her and slipped out of bed, grabbing my pajama pants from the floor as I went into the kitchen. Maybe a glass of wine would help still my thoughts.

I poured the wine and picked up my cell from the hall table before I headed into the living room. One missed call. I punched in my voicemail password, expecting a sales call or something equally wasteful of my time. I didn't get a lot of calls, especially after dinner. If there was an issue at the inn, Seth would handle it. He was proving to be a natural manager.

But it wasn't Seth. Instead, it was Keith Halford, my old friend who worked with me at the MGM in Vegas all those years ago, the only buddy I bothered to keep in touch with. His familiar voice filled the air and for a moment, I was lost in the memory of sharing a couple beers and war stories about some of the adventures we'd have to deal with managing a big hotel like the MGM, and I didn't bother to listen to what he was saying.

"*Opportunity.*" The word caught my attention, so I listened a little more carefully. And I was glad I did. I listened to the entire message once and then again.

"Leo, man. You can't miss out on this. I've stumbled on a

once-in-a-lifetime opportunity to get in on the ground floor of
something that's going to be huge."

My attention was definitely piqued by that detail alone, but
when Keith said what the opportunity was, I was definitely
excited.

"Lake Las Vegas," Keith's voice said. "What was supposed
to be a luxury resort is up for sale at a bargain. We need one
more investor. A manager."

A manager.

I was familiar with Lake Las Vegas. Anyone who worked in
the hotel industry in Vegas was definitely familiar with the
development that was meant to be a luxury destination for the
stars and wealthy of the world. Of course, that was before the
major economic crash when everything went to shit. I'd heard
rumors about some of the properties, but that was right around
the time I was starting my life in Canada with Lexi, and to be
honest, it wasn't really on my radar. But what Keith was saying
was definitely on my radar. Especially the word opportunity.
That one kept playing over and over in my head.

I couldn't ignore it. There was no way I could take him up
on any kind of opportunity, no matter how good it was, but I still
had to know what it was. It was late, but he'd be up. Keith never
slept either.

Sure enough, he picked up on the third ring.

"You got my message."

I grinned at his direct greeting. "I did. Sounds interesting."

"More than interesting, Leo. It's a once-in-a-lifetime
opportunity. I'm telling you. You *need* to see this place."

I chuckled and shook my head, even though he couldn't see
me. "I don't know, Keith. What's the point?"

"The point is that you would be a friggin' moron to miss out
on this. I know you, Leo. I know what you can do and I *know*
you need to be part of this project."

"Keith, man. I live in Canada now. I'm not there."

"You could be here."

I didn't respond right away because there was nothing I could say. It was true. I *could* be there. "Look, I—"

"Just come see it," he interrupted me. "Come and see the opportunity before you say no. You owe that to yourself. At the very least."

I nodded and I don't know whether it was the late hour, the lack of sleep, or the fact that I'd just had the love of my life in my arms, but I said yes. "Okay."

"Okay?"

I nodded again, more for my own benefit than his. "Yeah. I'll come visit and check it out." There was nothing to be gained by going to see what I'd be missing out on, but I just couldn't say no. Besides, maybe I could convince Lexi to come on a little vacation with me. Maybe even take Ben and show him where his mother and I met. It could be good for us.

No.

It *would* be good for us. Very good.

CHAPTER THREE

~Lexi~

There was nothing I hated more than sitting on the cold vinyl table in the doctor's office so that my bare thighs that weren't covered by the flimsy paper gown stuck to the surface uncomfortably. No. There was nothing I hated quite that much, unless, of course, it was sitting on that table in a thin gown waiting for the doctor to come in and tell me what I already knew but wasn't sure I wanted confirmed.

The wait was torturous. I looked at the clock for at least the tenth time, but it still showed only five minutes had gone by. Not the thirty it felt like. The paper gown scratched at my neck. I tugged at it, trying in vain to make it a little more comfortable. I was just about to give up and pull my clothes on when there was a knock on the door and it opened.

"Lexi?" Dr. Colbert walked into the room. A woman not much older than me, her smile warm and friendly, I could imagine we'd be friends under different circumstances. As it was, it was hard to be friends with someone who routinely gave you bad news. It was a bit of a friendship killer.

I nodded in greeting and bit my bottom lip. I already knew what she was going to tell me. I took the pregnancy test the day before. It was positive, just as I knew it would be but I'd somehow managed to talk myself into ignoring the result until it could be confirmed by the doctor. Pregnancy tests weren't always effective and with any luck, it was wrong. Or maybe it was right. I no longer knew what I wanted the answer to be.

Positive or negative?

Either way, the end result would be the same.

No baby.

"How are you, Lexi?" Dr. Colbert perched on her stool, clipboard in her hand. I was going to rip it out of her hand and check the file myself if she didn't just tell me what I wanted to know. Positive or negative. One word. That's all I needed out of her.

"Honestly?" I took a deep breath and tried to force a smile but there was no point. "I'm a little nervous." I nodded with my head to her clipboard and she smiled.

"Understandably so." The doctor flipped through a few papers before she looked at me again. "I think you already know what the results were."

The air left my lungs in a whoosh and a flutter of excitement lit up deep in my stomach. I guess I did know what I wanted the answer to be. A smile so wide I could feel it tug at my cheeks crossed my face. But there was that twinge of worry there, too. A big twinge. A really, *really* big twinge. The smile faltered a little and Dr. Colbert noticed.

"Lexi, I don't want you to worry, okay?"

How could I not?

"I mean it. Worry isn't good for the baby. You need to try to reduce stress and just carry on as normal, okay?"

I nodded, but in my head I mentally listed all the ways I couldn't possibly reduce stress at that moment and then I immediately felt guilty about doing that, because that was stressful, too.

"Lexi." I focused on the doctor who stared at me, concern etched across her face. "Stop. I really need you to stop."

"It's hard." I sucked my lip between my teeth again and bit down to keep from crying. The situation was too messed up. I was supposed to be excited. Pregnancy was supposed to be a time of celebration, not concern.

The doctor flipped open her chart and scribbled. "I'm sure it's very hard, but we've run all the tests and there's no reason that your body shouldn't be able to carry a healthy pregnancy to term. That being said, I do think it's prudent to take a few precautions. Try to rest, as I said; reduce stress if possible; maybe spend some time with your family just relaxing and enjoying yourself. What about a vacation? There's a few days off of school coming up, isn't there? Why not get away for a bit?"

It wasn't a bad idea. And there was a small school holiday scheduled for next week. Plus I had a few personal days to use up and Ben's birthday was right around the corner. But where would we go? A holiday was a good idea in theory, but—

"Consider it," Doctor Colbert said. "Even to let yourself adjust to the idea of the pregnancy. You should never underestimate the power of positive thinking. Based on the dates you gave me, I'd say you're just past twelve weeks. That's longer than any of the other pregnancies. In fact, I'd hesitantly say you're out of the danger zone. Why did you wait so long before coming in?"

We both knew the answer to that question. I'd become more than a little cautious when it came to pregnancy. She didn't push me on the point, instead adding, "We should schedule an ultrasound. I'd like to get a look at the little one and make sure our dates are on. Based on your history, and the fact that your periods haven't been all that regular over the last year or so, there's a chance our dates are wrong. Should we schedule the ultrasound for two weeks from now? That would give you a chance to take that little holiday we were talking about."

I nodded again. I started to feel like a bobblehead. I would consider it. I would consider doing anything that would help this pregnancy. I wasn't sure I could handle going through the loss again. And if I really was so far along...could it...maybe?

"Good. Here's another prescription for prenatal vitamins. Lots of water and healthy food and plenty of rest. But you know all that." I nodded and she moved to stand up. "And Lexi, honestly, it will be okay. Just live your life. The human body is extremely resilient, and sometimes you just need to trust."

I sat on the table for a few minutes longer after she left the room, the prescription clutched in my hand. My eyes blurred with unshed tears but I knew she was right. I had to think positively and I would, too. But I'd do it quietly. At least until after the ultrasound. My hand fluttered to my belly and I let my fingers dance across the paper gown. Yes, I think this baby would be my little secret. At least for now.

~Leo~

I WAS TAKING a risk by planning everything before I talked to Lexi, but once I got the idea in my head, I couldn't shake it. Besides, it had been way too long since I'd surprised her with anything. It wasn't too hard to arrange the details. With the school holiday coming up, all I needed to do was talk to Principal Henderson and let him know Lexi would need a few extra days off, which turned out to be easier than I thought because Lexi never took a day off.

Principal Henderson promised to keep everything quiet until I had a chance to tell her myself. I'd left a note for Ben's teacher, Liz, to put together a few assignments for Ben to make up while he was gone. He'd only miss a few days, but still, I didn't want there to be any excuse for Lexi to reject the trip. If I took care of all the details, she'd have to go along with it and even more than that, she'd be able to relax and enjoy herself. And that, more than anything, was what I wanted. The last few years, a seriousness—almost like a deep concern—had settled over my beautiful girl, and I needed to bring back the light in her eyes for good. I knew she probably wouldn't think so right away, but returning to Vegas would do that. I was sure of it. And I'd prove it to her.

Once the details at the school were confirmed, the only thing left to do was buy the tickets. So I did that, too. And then I printed them out, put them in an envelope and tucked them into my computer case. I didn't really have a plan for asking Lexi—or more specifically, telling her—about the trip, but I wasn't too worried about it. There were still a few details I needed to take care of as far as the inn was concerned.

I grabbed a sweater and left my office behind in search of Seth. A manager was only as good as his employees, and with Seth, I knew I had it good. He could handle pretty much anything I threw at him. Not that I'd given him anything particularly challenging, but that was about to change. Since taking over the Lake Lillian Inn, I'd never taken a vacation. Sure, a day or two here and there, but I'd never left the inn in someone else's hands before. That was about to change.

"Seth." I found the man chopping wood at the back of the inn. This time of year, things were slow and there weren't many guests, so it was a good time to take care of some of the more basic jobs. Especially before the snow flew. We'd need all that wood, and more.

The other man finished his swing before he propped up his ax, wiped his forehead with his sleeve and grabbed the logs. "Hey, boss. What's up?" He tossed the logs easily onto the stack he'd been building and walked over to where I waited. "I'm finished back here for today. Is there something you want me to take care of?"

"Actually, there is." I gestured to the maintenance shed. "Let's go chat." It had been Seth's idea to keep a fridge stocked with refreshments in the shed, and it had proved to be a fantastic idea on more than one occasion as we'd held impromptu meetings there. The beauty of owning a small operation was the relaxed approach we could take. It was definitely one of the perks and on days when I missed the chaos and busyness of Las Vegas, I tried to remember that small town hotel management also had distinct benefits.

I pulled two cans from the fridge and tossed him one before I leaned back against the work bench.

"Everything okay, Leo?"

I cracked the can and took a long pull. "Absolutely. I just need to talk to you about something." He nodded, so I continued. "I'm going to be taking a bit of a trip and I need to know if you'll be okay on your own for a few days."

He didn't answer right away, but instead rolled the can in his hands and took a deep drink. When he'd had a minute to think it over, he answered. "Of course. Is there any reason you think I wouldn't be okay? Do you not trust my abilities?"

Dammit. The last thing Leo needed was to offend his right-hand man. Especially before leaving him in charge. But before he could say anything or work on damage control, the corners of Seth's eyes crinkled with laughter and he slapped his knee. "Just pulling your chain, boss. Of course I'm good. What's going on?"

I shot him a quick look and shook my head before filling him in on what I had planned for Lexi. He wholeheartedly approved of my plan and even offered to take the dog. One detail I'd overlooked with all my arrangements. We spent another beer discussing what needed to be done for the busy holiday season that would be upon us before we knew it. By the time I left him, Seth was excitedly making plans for his time in charge and I knew I'd made a good decision. Not only would the inn be in good hands with him, I was certain he'd thrive with the responsibility.

Now there was only one thing left to do. Tell Lexi.

Her car was parked in front of the house when I pulled up next to it. I grabbed my laptop bag, the tickets tucked inside, and went to find her.

She was gorgeous. As soon as I saw her standing in front of the sink, my body responded. Just looking at her beauty made my stomach flip and my groin tighten and damned if I didn't want to take her in my arms, lift her onto the counter and kiss her until she made that sexy little moan of hers. It took all the restraint I had to hold back. There'd be time for that soon enough. First, I had to—a sigh escaped her lips in response to whatever she was watching outside. It wasn't a happy or content sigh, but one laced with concern and heaviness.

I followed her gaze outside to see what she was looking at, but there was nothing there but the lake. Not quite cold enough to freeze over, the water had started to crystallize. It would only be a matter of days before it was solid. A state of change that always made me a little sad, because try as I might, I could not get used to winter in the mountains. There was no amount of preparation that could prepare a man for that. Especially a man who grew up in the desert. But that didn't explain the melancholy on Lexi's face.

I slid up behind her, and wrapped my arms around her

waist to pull her close. She jumped a bit, startled by my presence, but settled in against my chest; her head fell back so I could drop a kiss on her forehead.

"What are you thinking about?" I stroked my hands down her arms. My fingers trailed back up before I rubbed her shoulders gently to work out the knots of tension that were always there.

"I'm good," she said. "Just a little tired is all." She turned in my arms and looked up at me. "That feels good. Thank you."

"Only the best for you, babe." It was the perfect segue. "I've noticed you've been tired a lot lately." She opened her mouth to protest, but I cut her off. "I know you've been working a lot and with everything going on the last little while, it's totally understandable. But, I think it's long past time we did something about it. Don't you?"

Confusion clouded her eyes. "I don't—"

"I've been thinking. We need to get away."

"Away? Where?" She didn't immediately say no, which was the answer I'd been expecting, so I took her question as a positive. A *big* positive. "It's not like we have anywhere to go, Leo. And what about Ben?"

"Ben will come, too, of course."

"Come where?" She tilted her head and narrowed her eyes as she pulled away just far enough to look me up and down. "What are you talking about, Leo?"

I smiled. I couldn't help it. The excitement was too much. This was exactly what we needed right now. That had never been so clear as it was at that moment.

I held her at arm's length so I could see her face when I told her the news. She'd be thrilled because why wouldn't she? I planned every detail. Took care of everything. All she had to do was pack a bag and get on the plane. And if there's anything I knew about Lexi, I knew she loved it when I took control of things.

"You're scaring me."

I laughed. "Why would I be scaring you?"

"The smile on your face..." She looked at me sideways but I could see her own smile forming on her lips. I was infecting her with my excitement. I could see it. "It's very suspicious."

I laughed again, louder this time, and gave her a deep, very thorough kiss on the lips before I pulled her away again.

"Leo, what is going on?"

"We're going on a trip." I couldn't keep it in any longer. But instead of looking excited the way I expected her to, the smile that had been forming on Lexi's face fell. I continued quickly. "And before you can think of any objections or arguments about where we would go or when, don't worry about a thing."

Lexi tugged out of my grasp, but I pulled her back and wrapped my arms around her.

"What are you talking about?" She looked up at me, so many questions in her eyes. "What shouldn't I worry about? The very fact that you say that..."

"I planned it all, babe." I thought the smile would crack my face in two. "Pack your bags because tomorrow morning we're leaving for Las Vegas."

CHAPTER FOUR

~Lexi~

Vegas.

Vegas.

Of all the places for him to book a surprise trip, he had to pick Vegas. I mean, I understood. Sort of. Okay, not really at all. I hated Vegas. Well, hate was a strong word. I didn't feel as strongly about Sin City as I used to, but old feelings died hard. And sure, Leo and I reconnected in Las Vegas, but we'd also been torn apart there so many years ago. There were a lot of memories in that city. Not all of them good.

But most of them, the little voice in the back of my head told me for the dozenth time. I'd long since given up on sleep. There was no way it was going to happen anyway, not with so many feelings floating around my head. Not the least of which was that I was supposed to try to eliminate stress. Not increase it. But Dr. Colbert had said a vacation would be a good thing. I don't think she meant a stressful vacation, but still, it was a vacation and according to Leo, I didn't have to worry about a thing except packing some clothes, which I'd managed to do in a few hours.

But now, while the house was quiet, the men in my life no doubt dreaming of warmer temperatures and jumping into a pool, all I could feel was a numbness that was occasionally permeated by a blast of panic. There was something about Vegas that I couldn't shake.

I pulled the sweater around my body and opened the door that led to the porch. The blast of autumn air hit me and knocked me back a step. Winter really was coming. It was too cold to be outside, but it didn't matter. I welcomed the cold air that numbed my toes and froze my nose. I needed something to knock me out of the mood I was in.

I felt guilty that I hadn't told Leo about the baby. We told each other everything, and the secret weighed on me, but I had to stick to my original plan. I wouldn't say anything until after the ultrasound confirmed everything was okay. And that would be after the trip.

The trip.

Yes, I'd let him have the trip that he was obviously so excited about before I told him anything. The opportunity for it to end the way all the others had was just too high. I'd wait.

Until after the trip.

The trip. I tried not to audibly sigh. I needed to control my feelings.

"It'll be a good thing." I spoke to the moon and watched my breath come out in puffs as I spoke. I said it again. And then again.

By the third time I vocalized the words, I almost believed them. I shook my head and wrapped my arms tighter around myself. It really would be a good thing. Ben was so excited when

Leo told him about going to Vegas and how we'd show him where we'd met and the hotel he used to work at.

I was pretty sure he was more excited about the heat and swimming in a pool as well as just generally seeing the spectacle that was Las Vegas. It wasn't hard to win Ben over to the idea of a vacation.

"And it shouldn't be hard for you either, Lexi."

I'd definitely sunk to a new level of crazy if I was talking to myself, but I didn't care. It was helping. I was right. It shouldn't be hard to win me over to the idea of a trip. Besides, it wasn't really Las Vegas we were going to, but Lake Las Vegas, which I'd never heard of but Leo told me was about thirty minutes off the Strip. He had a buddy who was running a hotel there and had gotten us a good deal. I knew there was more to the story, and my Spidey senses were on alert at the mention of Keith and a hotel he'd just started running, but it was one of the many things I needed to put out of my head. Especially if I was going to enjoy this trip.

And I would.

I owed it to my family and to myself. Besides, if a vacation was good for the baby, that's what I'd do. And maybe by the time we got back and were all rested and rejuvenated, everything would be back to normal: Leo would be content, Ben's friend issues at school would have benefited from a little distance, and the baby would be okay. Maybe, just maybe, a trip to Las Vegas was exactly what my family needed.

At least, that's what I was going to keep telling myself.

~Leo~

It had been five years since I'd been in the McCarran Airport, but aside from the different signs advertising whatever hot new show was playing on the Strip, it was exactly the same. The slot machines chimed and rang, as passengers got an early start on their visit to Sin City, or in some cases, a last-ditch effort to win back everything they'd lost. I loved it. I'd always loved it. I glanced over at Lexi and Ben walking next to me through the concourse and wasn't surprised to see the tight line of Lexi's lips. She'd never really understood Vegas and the gambling. The excess.

I remembered that first night we spent together. The night that changed everything and how I opened her eyes to everything Vegas could be. That had been different. We'd been different. I slipped my hand into hers and squeezed, tugging her a little closer to my side. This trip would be different, too. For me, Vegas was about the two of us and how we'd come together. Twice. We'd do it again, too. Only this time we'd come *back* together.

"This place is so cool." Ben's eyes danced all over the airport, taking in the flashing lights, slots, and hordes of people.

I laughed and put my hand on his shoulder as we stood in front of the baggage claim. "If you think this is cool, wait until you see the Strip. You'll be—"

"I didn't think we were going to the Strip."

Dammit. I forgot I'd promised that. I gave her a smile and kissed her cheek. "Of course."

Knowing her hesitancy about bringing Ben to Vegas in the first place, I'd promised her we'd keep him away from the debauchery that had a tendency to overwhelm the city. For Lexi, that included the Strip; for me, I was pretty sure we could find some kid-appropriate activities that Ben would like.

I lifted her hand to my mouth and dropped a kiss in her

palm before I curled her fingers over it. "It's going to be great, Lex. I promise."

She smiled, and it was a real smile. The beautiful, heart-stopping smile that melted me from the first moment I met her all those years ago.

I knew she wasn't excited about the trip. Of course she'd tried to pretend she was, but I could see there was something, a hesitancy of some kind, holding her back from really getting excited about it. It was Vegas. I wasn't dumb. Despite the fact that Vegas had given us...well, us, Lexi still struggled with the city. As if she was haunted by it. But that was going to change. Not only was I going to check out this opportunity Keith kept raving about—and he did, with multiple emails that outlined the details—but I was determined to get things back on line with Lexi. She was the best thing that had ever happened to me, but with every miscarriage, something inside her dimmed a little. It killed me to watch it happening, especially because as her light dimmed, there wasn't a damned thing I could do about it. I knew she wanted a baby more than anything and I knew it was because she felt she owed me the experience because I'd missed it with Ben. And yes, I'd welcome another member of our family, but not because I missed anything with Ben. I may not have met him until he was five but it didn't matter. He was an amazing kid and we still had a lifetime together. No, I did not want to increase our family at the expense of what it was doing to the woman I loved. And I'd tell her that, too. It was time for a new start. No more baby talk. I couldn't watch her go through it again. I was a strong man, but everyone had their kryptonite, and watching Lexi hurt was mine.

WHEN WE'D RETRIEVED our bags, I led my family to the doors and we were immediately hit by the desert heat. It was the middle of November but it was still hot in Nevada, at least during the day. And even if the locals were all wearing sweaters and jeans, it was a hell of a lot warmer than the Canadian Rockies.

"Keith arranged a car for us," I said at the same moment I saw the driver holding a sign that read "Mendez."

"A limo?" Ben gave a fist pump. "That's so cool, Dad." It had been five years, but hearing Ben calling me Dad never got old; neither did doing something he thought was cool. Although, as he got older, those moments came fewer and further between.

"Nothing but the best for you, buddy." I stopped myself moments before ruffling his hair and settled for a light punch to the shoulder. Lexi shook her head, but I could see the satisfied look on her face as we settled into the leather seats and I slid my hand up her thigh, secretly, so our son didn't see and make a face.

While Ben was busy checking out the features of the limo and choosing stations on the built-in satellite radio, I took the chance to lean into Lexi and whisper in her ear.

"Do you realize this is our first family holiday?"

"No." She shook her head and stared at me. "It can't be. We must have..." She drifted off but it only took her a moment to come to the same conclusion. "Wow. You're right. I can't believe that."

It was amazing how quickly time went by and we were long overdue for some family memories together. I was very aware that Lexi and her first husband, Andrew—The man whom she'd agreed to marry only days after meeting me. The man who'd raised my child for his first five years of his life, as his own, despite knowing that Ben couldn't possibly be his. The man who was living the life I should have had if I hadn't made one wrong decision that had kept me away from the love of my life that day—I was fully aware they'd had family holidays. Trips to

Mexican resorts with pools and waterslides every second winter. Disneyland to meet Mickey Mouse when Ben was four. Even a cruise in the Mediterranean when Ben was a baby. Lexi had shown me all the pictures. Not to make me jealous, or resentful of what I'd missed, but to fill me in on the details of Ben's life. And I hadn't been resentful or jealous either, but I'd be lying if I said I hadn't been dying to make some new memories as a real family. And now was the time.

"It's long overdue." I kissed her, soft and sweet. "And it's going to be great, Lex. Just what we need."

CHAPTER FIVE

~Lexi~

It took just over thirty minutes to get from the airport to Lake Las Vegas and by the time we got there, my anxiety level had dropped considerably. Leo was right. We'd never had a family holiday and we were long overdue. Besides, I didn't need to get all worked up about Vegas. If I really stopped to think about it, there were definitely more good memories than bad here. A lot more. Leo and I had met here. Ben was conceived here. Leo and I reconnected here. These were all good things. Very good things. I was being ridiculous.

Sometimes it took your best friend pointing that out for you to see it yourself. And that's exactly what happened the night before when I called Nicole to tell her about the trip.

"I'm so jealous," she'd moaned over the line. "Ryan and I would join you in a heartbeat if I wasn't big as a house." Nicole and Ryan were expecting their first child, right after Christmas. A fact that as her best friend, I was thrilled about. But as a woman who was desperate to have a baby of her own, stung a little every time we talked. "Oh God, Lexi. I'm sorry. I shouldn't have—"

"Of course you should have. My baby-less status has nothing to do with your big belly, and that's the way it should be. You know I'm thrilled for you guys. Besides, I can't wait to finally be Auntie Lexi and pay you back for all those obnoxious toys you gave Ben over the years."

Nicole's laughter filled the line, followed quickly by a small squeal. "Oh my God. How is it that I'm already peeing a little when I laugh? I thought that wasn't supposed to happen until after childbirth. This kid is going to be trouble. I already know it."

I laughed along with her. "Yes, she is. Especially if she's anything like you."

"No fair. I am amazing."

"Yes, you are." It was the truth. "But Ryan is definitely going to have his work cut out for him with two of you." Also the truth.

"Well, I know you can help with that. As her godmother, you'll be the perfect role model and pick up all my parenting slack."

I rolled my eyes, despite the fact she couldn't see. Nicole and I had been best friends since college and we'd always been polar opposites. Where she'd been outgoing and daring, I'd been quiet and reserved. But somehow it worked. She was the yang to my yin, a perfect balance. And when she and Ryan asked Leo and me to be the godparents to their child, despite the fact that we didn't attend church on a very regular basis—at all—there was no answer besides absolutely yes.

"About that," Nicole continued. "The minister asked again the other day about your marital status. What's going on there?"

The fact that Leo and I had never gotten around to getting

married seemed to bother almost everyone else more than it bothered us.

"You know," I'd said, "I think it's interesting how worried you are about Leo and me being legitimate godparents when you guys didn't even get married in a church."

"Well, first of all," Nicole said with a sigh. "You know that for us, the whole godparent thing is more about having a guardian and a special relationship with you than anything religious."

I knew that. We'd discussed it before.

"But it's important to Ryan's mom," Nicole continued. "Like, really important. And the more I think about it, I think it's probably a good idea. I mean, it can't hurt to secure things with the big guy upstairs, right?"

I laughed. That was typical Nicole and I loved her for it. "I get it, Nic. I do."

"So about the wedding?"

"There isn't a wedding." I tried not to sigh. "In fact, the reason I'm calling is to tell you that we're all going on a trip. Leo planned a little surprise long weekend thing to Lake Las Vegas."

"Vegas?"

"*Lake* Las Vegas." I emphasized *lake*. "It's a completely different place."

"Not if it has Vegas in the name."

Again, I rolled my eyes. "Whatever."

"How are you with that?" Nicole knew about my hang-ups when it came to Vegas. Of course, Nicole knew everything. That being said, she'd still dragged me back there for her wedding, which of course had been a good thing in hindsight. "Before you answer," she continued. "Because I know how you'll answer. And I'm fairly positive you're being ridiculous. So, I just want you to think about all the good stuff that's happened there. And how really, it's your special place. I know you like to think about the reasons you should never go back. But instead, why don't you think about all the reasons you *should*? Besides that, if anyone needs a vacation, it's you guys. I know things have been rough lately." Her voice got quiet and I knew she was trying hard not to cry, something she did a lot since becoming pregnant. "You guys all deserve to relax and reconnect as a family."

She had no idea. I'd opened my mouth to tell her about the positive pregnancy test, but I closed it and swallowed my secret. What was the point? The only thing sharing the information would do was get everyone's hopes up again. Only to dash them in a few weeks. No. I'd keep my secret to myself.

In the end, I'd hung up the phone with Nicole, feeling slightly better, but mostly determined. I would enjoy this holiday.

We drove through the small village that was Lake Las Vegas, a village made up of mostly palatial homes backing on golf courses and a main village square area lined with cobblestone streets, boutiques, coffee shops, and restaurants. When we turned a corner and the lake came into view, Ben shrieked.

"There are paddle boards out there. It's not frozen."

Leo laughed. "No, buddy, this lake doesn't freeze."

The look on Ben's face was priceless. Of course he was old enough to know in theory that there were lakes in the world that didn't freeze. He just hadn't seen any.

"It doesn't freeze? Like, ever?"

"Like ever. It gets a bit cooler in the winter. So you might not want to swim in January or February. But you—"

"I could if I wanted to?" Ben's eyes were wide. Growing up at the lake, especially in the last few years, had turned my boy into a water baby. If it involved water, Ben couldn't get enough of it.

"Yes you could," Leo said with another laugh.

"Except, of course, it's November now," I added quickly. Something in Leo's eyes made me nervous. "And we won't be here in January."

He looked away quickly. But not before I saw a flash of something else in his eyes. *Want?* Desire to be back in the desert? I couldn't know. And it wasn't something I wanted to explore. Not right then. Besides, there was no time.

The car slowed and turned down a long drive. We all stopped talking and stared out the windows as the car made its way toward what could have been a very posh resort hotel. Whoever had built it had an eye for the posh life. Marble columns flanked the main doors, which looked to be a solid wall of glass, surrounded by oversize fountains and pools that were currently and strangely, empty. I could see how the grounds could be magnificent if they were cared for. As they were, the grass was brown, the flower gardens full of mostly weeds and dirt. Something wasn't right.

I looked to Leo, confused. He'd said his buddy had given them a good deal on the resort, but this place looked absolutely abandoned. There were only a few cars in the parking lot and no staff in sight.

"What is this—"

"Look. There's Keith." Leo diverted my attention. The car pulled up in front of the main doors and a man who looked vaguely familiar opened the door.

"Welcome to Oasis!"

Ben turned to look at us. I shrugged, and Leo gestured to the door so he scrambled quickly outside. Leo followed and held his hand back for me. The second I stepped out into the sunshine and saw the look on Leo's face as he scanned the desolate hotel, a small smile playing at his lips, a twinkle of excitement in his eyes, I knew. It was the same look he had on his face when he'd told me he bought the Lake Lillian Inn.

I still didn't know exactly what was going on. But one thing I knew for sure: our little family vacation had just gotten a lot more interesting.

~Leo~

I NEEDED to take a minute just to look around and take it all in. Keith was right. The place was a perfect opportunity. And I could see that after only five minutes through the door. Without hearing any of the specifics, I knew this empty shell of a hotel could be fantastic. No, it *would* be fantastic.

"This place is so cool!" Ben ran past me for the second time as he explored the lobby, a cavernous room lined with polished marble floors, a vaulted ceiling, and what must have been the shell for a fountain in the middle of the space.

"It is pretty cool."

"You should see the outside," Keith told him. "My girlfriend's kids, Evan and Ruby, are out there. I think they're about your age. Go say hi."

Ben turned and gave Lexi a look.

She only shrugged and waved. "Go. But be careful."

"He'll be fine. There's not much trouble he can get into out here," Keith said. "And really, you guys need to see the outside. That's where the magic really is. Come on."

I knew there would be a thousand questions running through Lexi's head by now and the fact that she hadn't voiced any of them yet both gave me hope and made me nervous as hell. It wasn't my intention to deceive her. But I needed to get down here and see the opportunity for myself. More than that, I needed her to see it, too.

She started to follow Keith out the huge glass doors that led out to what I could already see were amazing grounds, but I grabbed her hand and pulled her back. Over Lexi's shoulder, I could see Keith look back in question. But he was no fool. It only took him a second to see we needed a moment. He nodded and smiled and took off down the path. We'd find him in a minute.

I spun Lexi into me and held her in a tight hug until I could feel her body loosen against me. After a moment, she asked the question I knew was on her mind.

"This place. This is why we're really here?"

"No." I didn't want to lose the feel of her against my body, but I needed to look into her eyes and make damn sure she understood what I was about to say. "It was a reason to come," I explained slowly. "But it absolutely was *not* why I wanted to get away with you and Ben. We needed this." I ran my hand over her head and brushed a stray strand of hair from her cheek. "Lexi..."

She took my hand in hers and held it to her lips. "I know, Leo. It's okay."

"It is?" I asked the question, but I knew the answer.

She nodded her affirmation. "I wish you would have told me the truth, though. If I would have known I was going to have a holiday in an empty hotel, I might have packed differently."

She laughed and in that moment it was as if the years melted away and the stress of real life—our life and everything we'd been through that had made my love so sad—vanished and she was happy again. Maybe it was the place? Maybe it was Vegas? It was too soon to tell. I definitely needed more time to figure out what the deal was with the hotel before I started down that road, but there was definitely a shift within her. And I liked it. I liked it a lot.

Lexi ran her fingers down my back and I tilted my head down to take her lips in mine. The kiss wasn't long enough, but there'd be time for more later. "Should we go see why Keith is so excited about the outdoor space?"

Her smile lit up her face. "Absolutely. And then maybe later we could find some time to be alone?"

Yes. I definitely liked this shift in her.

~Lexi~

I WASN'T STUPID. There was definitely a reason Leo had brought us to an empty shell of a hotel. And I'm almost positive it had something to do with him wanting to run it. Or at least Keith wanting him to run it. Either way, I could see right away that Leo was worried about my reaction. Hell, I was worried about my reaction. But surprisingly, I wasn't upset. It was easy to see the way his face lit up when he looked around the empty lobby. Whatever was going on with the hotel, Leo was in his element. He loved a challenge and this was definitely that.

"You're pretty amazing." He gave me another kiss and looked me deep in the eyes, no doubt trying to figure out what had gotten into me.

"You can stop looking at me like that." I laughed and it felt good. "Honestly, I'm fine." And surprising even myself, I was. "Come on."

I dragged him toward the door and the oversized patio on the other side. The whole wall was made up of windows that could open, giving the already huge room an inside/outside feel. The lake was just beyond, glittering in the desert sun. It was very different than the mountain lake I was used to, but there was a different kind of beauty to the sparkling water, and I could easily see the appeal of jumping in on a hot day. An oasis in the desert. The name of the resort was perfect.

"Mom!" Ben's voice yanked me back to the scene in front of me. "You have got to see this pool." I turned to where he stood at the water's edge, practically jumping up and down from the excitement. He was such a water baby, I could only laugh and shake my head. It was clear he was desperate to get in and go swimming and I couldn't blame him. It was one of the coolest pools I'd seen: a lazy river wrapped around the outside; the pool itself was graduated in depth, surrounded by lush gardens and lawns with a waterfall at one end. The outdoor space was in direct contrast to the unfinished indoors.

"It looks pretty awesome." I joined Ben on the edge of the pool and put my hand on his shoulder. "You should join them." I nodded toward the two other children, who did look awfully similar in age to Ben. They floated on tubes around the lazy river. If you could call it floating. Mostly they were pushing each other off, diving under, splashing, and just being kids.

"Can I?"

"Of course you can." It was Leo who spoke, but it was the only invitation Ben needed. "Go."

"There's a change house over there, buddy. And Evan has his extra suits in there. He's about your size." Keith pointed just behind them where there was a small outbuilding almost completely surrounded by lush vegetation. "Go change. Ruby and Evan will grab you a tube." He whistled and waved the kids over. As they made their way through the water, Ben took off to get ready and I wandered around the pool's edge, taking in everything there was to see.

And there was a lot to see.

Besides the pool we stood beside, there was more. A lap pool was tucked a little farther down a path. That pool was fed by the lazy river and a fountain that spilled into one end. An elaborate stream-like system continued from that pool and trailed down toward the lake and what resembled a tropical sandy beach.

Without even knowing I was doing it, I found myself walking toward the beach. I kicked my sandals off and sunk my toes into the silky sand that covered my feet like a warm blanket. It was incredible. If I didn't know better, I would have thought I was in the Caribbean. Palm trees surrounded the beach area and chaise lounge chairs were scattered about. I drifted closer to the water and was about to test the temperature when Keith's voice stopped me.

"Incredible, isn't it?"

I turned and smiled. If someone would have told me I'd be smiling only hours after landing in Las Vegas, I would have told them how crazy they were. But I was. And the smiles were genuine because I didn't feel the anxiety I thought I would. But this wasn't Vegas. This was...

"It is incredible," I agreed and turned back toward the lake. People were stand up paddle boarding around the shoreline, with a few braver souls headed out into the middle of the lake. There were a number of kayaks scattered across the surface as well. But no power boats. "It's oddly peaceful."

Keith stepped up so he stood next to me. "Right? Because there are only a handful of power boats allowed on the lake, and those are gondola style that don't go very fast. In fact, there are a lot of regulations, mostly surrounding the wind. But I guess that's what keeps it so calm and safe."

"Wind?"

Keith nodded. "It can get pretty windy in the desert, and quickly, too. So when the wind speed hits a certain point, a call goes out and they shut it down. It keeps everything really safe and then there aren't any worries about accidents because, let's face it," he grinned, his teeth flashing in the sun, "an accident history tends to put a damper on vacation bookings. No one wants to die while they're on holidays."

"I suppose not." I shook my head and laughed a little. "So what's going on with this place?" There was no point beating around the bush with him. I wasn't dumb or blind and there was clearly some reason we were there. And it was more than a *holiday*. Much more. I might as well find out what it was right away.

"Right to the point, aren't you?"

"You know me." In fact, he didn't. But that didn't really matter. "Why are we here?"

"Leo always said you were pretty straightforward."

"No point in anything else." I sunk my toes further in the sand. The action relaxed me as the grains slid over my skin. "So?"

Keith sighed next to me. I waited while he exhaled a long breath. "The original investors designed Lake Las Vegas to be an upscale destination for the wealthy who liked to visit Vegas, but wanted a bit of a more 'posh' experience." He held up his hands in air quotes. "The handful of separate investors signed on to build big resorts on this side of the lake, while the rest was for private development." I followed where he pointed to the mansions that dotted the hillside across the lake. "Celine Dion has a spot over there, with a helipad so she can get easily to and from the Strip for her shows." I raised my eyebrows, but didn't interrupt him. "Anyway," he continued. "Everything was going well until 2008 and the bottom more or less fell out of the economy and the luxury hotel market. This place was half finished when the shit hit the fan, and the financial backers just walked away. Which means—"

"An opportunity."

"Exactly."

"What about the other resorts?" I'd seen a few of the other

hotels as we drove in, and although they didn't seem to be the posh and elegant properties Keith was describing, they did have cars in the parking lots and seemed to have some action going on. "They didn't go under?"

He shook his head. "They were further along in development at the time and the property planners were smart. They scaled back a bit and adjusted their target market. The original investors of the Oasis didn't react quickly enough and finally it was easier just to walk away than to adapt."

"And you come in, how?" He still hadn't told me why we were there, but it was becoming clearer.

He ran his hand through his thick blond hair. He was a good-looking man; he oozed charisma, in a completely different way than Leo did. But still, it was easy to see why he was in the industry he was. "Obviously, there are new investors," he started. "But they wanted to do things with a different model." I raised an eyebrow. "They thought it would be best if they had managers who were invested."

"Invested?" There it was. In that one word.

"Obviously, it's a much smaller financial investment on the part of the managers."

"Obviously." I spoke as if I knew what I was talking about, but I had no idea what type of investment it would take to be part of such a grand operation. And more to the point, what it meant for Leo and me.

"We're really moving along." Keith kept talking. "You can see that we went after the exterior finishing first. At least in the back; the front is next on the list. It's important to establish the landscaping early because it gives everything a chance to take root and by the time the busier summer season hits, there will be lush lawns and—"

"Get to the point, Keith."

"It's a good opportunity, Lexi." Keith didn't miss a beat. "To get in on the ground level of something like this. Opportunities like this don't come along every day. I knew Leo would want to consider it."

And that was it. I'd known it from the moment the limo had pulled up in front of Oasis and I'd looked into Leo's eyes. This was just the type of challenge that got him excited. But...there were so many buts.

"How much?"

Keith shook his head and looked at me in question. "What do you mean?"

"You said there was a buy-in." I wrapped my arms around my abdomen. There was no way this could be something Leo would actually consider. Not without talking to me. Particularly if there were a financial investment involved. Because that was simply laughable. We didn't have any finances to invest. *Except, maybe we did...* I shook the thought clear from my head and focused on Keith's answer, almost wishing I hadn't.

"Two hundred and fifty."

"Two hundred and fifty?"

"Thousand," he clarified, as if I hadn't already figured that part out.

I swallowed against the lump in my throat and nodded carefully, as if I was considering what he'd just told me. But on the inside, I screamed, because despite the fact that in the grand scheme of things, it was an incredibly small amount, it was also a ridiculously huge amount and there was no way we could buy in to such an investment. Even if I was willing to consider uprooting my entire family to move back to the city that had always been my nemesis—which I wasn't—such a thing couldn't happen. Ever. Leo knew that.

Except...

I turned around to where Leo still stood by the pool, his hands on his hips, taking in the grounds. Even from the distance

I was at, I could see the way he held his head up, surveying everything. The grounds that could be his kingdom. I knew even without seeing the look in his eyes exactly what I would see there if I was close enough to see.

Excitement.

Passion.

Two of the things I hadn't seen in my love's eyes for a very long time.

But we didn't have that type of money.

Except we did.

I looked back at Keith, who watched me closely. I forced a smile and tried to appear as casual as I could.

I needed to talk to Leo.

~Leo~

"So you're in?" Keith held his hand out to me. Despite the fact that we'd been going over the pros and cons of buying in to the Oasis for the last hour and I had yet to find a flaw in the business plan, I didn't take his hand. We'd discussed changing the focus of the resort away from the original intention of being a posh, upscale destination, to a family-friendly vacation hot spot. "Leo?" Keith raised his eyebrow, but kept his hand extended. "You in? Or out?"

I may not have found a flaw in the business plan, but I'd definitely found a flaw in one minor—no, strike that—major detail. Lexi.

"You know Lexi's on board." It was as if he read my mind. "I talked to her," Keith continued. "She sees the potential."

I was sure she did. But I couldn't imagine she was on board. "I need to talk it over with her."

"I don't think you do." Keith shoved his hand in his back pocket. "I didn't need to discuss it with Roxanne. We're not married. My money is mine. My opportunities are mine. My future is—"

"Your own?" It was my turn to shake my head at him. "It will be your own if you keep taking that kind of attitude."

Keith shook his head and grabbed his beer. While we'd been going over the finer details of the agreement and the opportunity while Keith's girlfriend showed Lexi the spa and the suites at the back of the resort. Keith and his crew had taken up residence in one, and another would be for myself, Lexi, and Ben to stay in. At least for the time being. Maybe permanently? I couldn't get ahead of myself. As much as I loved being back in Nevada, the dry heat even in November seeping into my bones, it wasn't our home. And there was definitely more than just myself to consider. I needed to think about Lexi and Ben. My family. I could no longer make decisions without consulting my—

"Leo, look. I'm not trying to pressure you." I turned back to Keith, who looked exactly as though he was trying to pressure me. "But I told the investors you were a sure thing. If you're not interested, I need to start searching for someone who is. And I mean, like right now. I already told you the timeline for this. The soft launch will start December 20. In time for Christmas and we have some exciting things planned for the New Year so Oasis can come onto the scene in a big way. But I can't go ahead with any of that until I know if you're in or not. So what is it?"

I glanced around, hoping Lexi might appear around the corner and I could use the opportunity for a quick conversation. This was not a decision I could make on my own. I just couldn't.

"Leo."

Or could I?

It would be tight, but I knew Lexi had money set aside from

her uncle's estate. But I couldn't touch that. There was our savings. I know Lexi planned to have the cabin re-insulated. But if we moved, we wouldn't need to do that. I didn't have much saved, but I had a retirement savings from my days working on the Strip, and if I sold the Lake Lillian Inn...I could do it. But I'd have to sell the inn. I couldn't just move my whole family from the Canadian mountains to the Nevada desert without so much as a conversation with Lexi, could I?

But I'd seen the look in her eyes. I couldn't remember the last time I'd seen her looking so relaxed. So at peace. Maybe it was a chance for a fresh start for us as a family. A family of three. Back where it all began.

Vegas.

We could put all the baby talk out of our heads and focus on building a business together, as a family. I didn't need another child. I needed my family whole and happy and maybe the Oasis was exactly the place for that. I took a quick glance around at the pools where Ben was still playing with his new friends. I scanned the gardens that were just starting to take root, and let my eyes travel down to the water and the lake that was really the centerpiece for the resort. It was amazing. It could be great. That much I knew.

"Well?"

I turned my attention back to Keith.

"I'll do it." I thrust my hand out and he caught it quickly in his firm grip, solidifying our agreement.

CHAPTER SIX

~Lexi~

The first day passed quickly. Leo stayed up late chatting with Keith, but I could barely keep my eyes open. After a lovely dinner with everyone, I made my excuses and retreated to the suite, where I fell into a deep sleep almost the moment my head hit the pillow.

The next morning, I woke up feeling better than I had in ages. Relaxed and happy. Maybe that was why, when over breakfast, Leo suggested we go on a date night just the two of us, I said yes. I think I surprised both of us with my quick response, especially when he told me he wanted to visit the Strip.

I don't know why, but it felt okay. And Nicole was right: I couldn't continue hating a place for no reason. It was time for new memories.

I was confident that Ben was in good hands with Keith, Roxanne, and their kids, who had become instant friends for him. I slipped into my fanciest dress, which quite honestly wasn't all that fancy at all: a sky-blue halter dress that draped just enough to hide the extra pounds I'd put on over the last few years. I'd bought it for a wedding the summer before, and it was one of the few things in my closet that still fit, especially considering my breasts seemed to have swelled over the last few weeks. I tried not to put any merit into that fact, or put any pressure on the pregnancy that was still very much my little secret. But maybe if my body was changing, that was a positive sign?

No. I needed to put it out of my head. Time would tell the story, and there was nothing I could do about it until then. For the moment, I was determined to enjoy a romantic night out with Leo. It was long overdue.

We took the same limo that had brought us to the resort. Keith had arranged for dinner reservations and tickets for us to see *Jersey Boys* at the Paris hotel.

But before the show, Leo promised me dinner. When we walked into Planet Hollywood, he led me to Gordon Ramsay's upscale hamburger restaurant. Laughter ripped through me.

"It's perfect, right?"

When I had myself under control, I nodded. "It couldn't be more perfect." He leaned down to kiss my cheek and warmth spread through me. All those years ago, when Leo and I first met, we'd gone out for late-night burgers on the Strip. It was one of my favorite memories of our time together in Vegas. "Did you—"

Leo nodded. "I told Keith we needed burgers. I wasn't really expecting anything quite this fancy, but I guess I should have known." He took my hand and squeezed. "Shall we?"

Dinner was fantastic; the burgers were definitely delicious, and a lot more upscale than the greasy diner we'd discovered all those years ago, but every bit as good. But the best part was the conversation between us. It was easy and it flowed and there was no talk of babies, or money, or anything serious, really. I knew it wasn't reality. Our reality was all of those things, including the resort and the potential investment Keith had told me about. We needed to talk about all of those things, but for the night, it was okay to pretend we didn't have any of that stress in our life. Not only was it okay, it was preferred. We needed a carefree evening more.

I didn't know where Leo's head was at when it came to Oasis, but I had my suspicions. I'd noticed the way he'd lit up taking in the project and the potential it held. But what I didn't know was what he was thinking as far as investing every dollar we had, and some we didn't really have. It was a conversation we were going to need to have but I also knew it wasn't going to be a talk we could have lightly. There'd be time for that later. I kept the conversation light and easy, the only remotely important topic being the mention of Nicole and Ryan's baby and her strong desire for us to be married. We both laughed it off the way we always did when it was brought up, and soon the topic was changed altogether.

After dinner, we had to hurry to make it to the show on time, and we slipped into the best seats in the house right before the curtain rose. Soon I found myself lost in the story and the music. Along with the audience, I cried, cheered, and laughed as the story of Frankie Valli and the Four Seasons unfolded. By the time the curtain fell and the lights came up, I was perfectly content and despite myself, I couldn't remember why I'd ever wanted to stay away from such a fantastic city.

With his hand on the small of my back, Leo led me through the crowds in the casino and outside to the Strip. The lights flashed and danced, music pulsed throughout the air, and the energy of the city made it feel alive.

"Is the car waiting for us?" I looked up and down, but the effort was futile considering there were cars and people everywhere and no way for me to figure out which one was for us.

"I was thinking maybe we didn't have to go back quite yet." He wrapped his arms around me, creating a cocoon around me, protecting me from the people flowing all around us. "It's still early and we've had such a great night. I don't want it to end."

I nodded as his lips crushed down on mine. If I could stand there with him, his strong arms wrapped around me, holding me tight, ignoring the world and all the things we needed to talk about, I'd be happy to stay all night.

~Leo~

EVERYTHING WAS PERFECT. No, better than perfect because I was with Lexi and we were back where it all began. It felt so right, as if all the stress and drama of the last few years just disappeared and we were us again. Was it Vegas? I knew it wasn't. But I couldn't help but think it had something to do with it.

"Come on," I said. "I have an idea."

She laughed, the sound filling me as we made our way through the crowds. I knew exactly where our destination was, but it didn't mean we weren't going to take our time getting there. We stopped to watch the dancing fountains in front of the Bellagio. I wrapped my arms around her and pressed her body into mine, exactly where it belonged. When I nuzzled her neck, the moan that escaped her lips was pure music to my ears. I let my hands travel down her hips, sliding along her thighs, but that's where I let it end. There'd be time for that later, and I still had plans for us.

The crowds had cleared a little bit by the time we made it to

Caesars Palace. Lexi paused when she realized what I had in mind. "Really?" She laughed again and her face lit up. "I haven't done this forever."

I knew she was on board for what I had in mind, so I put my hands on her hips and lifted her easily up on the marble statue where we could sit and watch the people walk by.

All those years ago, on our first night together, we'd sat in the very same spot together and watched the variety of tourists walking by, making up stories about all of them. It was one of my favorite memories of that night together, and for years after, I couldn't walk past Caesars Palace without thinking of the blonde beauty who'd stolen my heart in so many ways that night.

"What about that guy?" Lexi pointed to a young man, his eyes wide as he took in the happenings around him. "It's his first time in Vegas."

"It's his first time out of the bunker," I added. Lexi looked at me with a smirk, so I continued. "He was born underground in a bomb shelter in Illinois where he spent the first twenty-two years of life. His family was recently discovered and brought above ground after they were convinced that there hadn't been a nuclear war and the world was still safe."

"So now he's experiencing life for the first time, in all its Vegas glory," Lexi added. "And of course he'd never seen a woman before..."

"Besides his mother."

"Obviously." She nodded and gestured as the man turned to ogle a show girl who walked by with her tiny sequinned top, feathers jutting from her headpiece. "And now his hormones are raging out of control. He's going to introduce himself to that girl."

"They'll fall in love," I chimed in.

"And get married by Elvis in a twenty-four-hour chapel at

the end of the Strip."

"That's what we should do." The idea flew into my head and out of my mouth so quickly, I didn't have time to censor my thoughts. Lexi stared at me and her mouth dropped open. "I mean, not necessarily by Elvis, but the—"

"Married?"

I nodded. The idea felt right. Really right.

"On the Strip?"

"Yes." I jumped up as the brilliance of my idea sunk in. "Why not? We've been saying for years that we're going to get married but something always comes up. Why wait? It's been a perfect night—let's do it."

It was a perfectly logical thing to do. And I meant exactly what I said: everything had been perfect. From dinner to the show, and mostly to just spending time with Lexi and hearing her beautiful laugh, seeing her gorgeous smile. Okay, it had been almost perfect. The lingering task of telling Lexi I'd invested all of our money into the hotel was weighing over me, and I knew I should tell her. Hell, I should have told her about it right after I did it, or probably even before. But that wasn't the point. The point was, I couldn't remember the last time I'd seen her so free and happy. I couldn't remember the last time we'd just...let loose and had fun. It had been way too long and if I told her about the hotel and the money, all of that would disappear. And that was the last thing I wanted.

What I really wanted was to keep that gorgeous smile on her face, and to do that, I couldn't think of a better time to make her my wife. Of course, I expected her to object and list a million reasons why we should wait, or not do it all. Lexi was the logical one. The one who could list all the reasons we should absolutely not get married. Which was why I was so surprised when she jumped up next to me, kissed me hard on the lips and said, "Let's do it."

~Lexi~

THE SECOND I agreed to Leo's outrageous plan, I clapped my hand over my mouth. What was I saying? Married? In Vegas? It was pretty much the exact opposite of the wedding I wanted.

Or was it?

We'd been talking about the idea of getting married for years and I couldn't seem to commit to anything. Why was that?

I knew exactly what the problem was. A big wedding in a church with a giant overdone party wasn't my style. We'd thought about going to Mexico and tying the knot on the beach, but that wasn't my style either. So what was my style?

Our style.

Vegas.

It had always been Vegas. Lexi and Leo in Las Vegas.

It was perfect.

"Are you sure?"

I nodded and looked my love in the eyes. "Yes." I'd never been more sure. "I need a dress."

"You look perfect." My hands flew to my hair and smoothed down my head. "Honestly, you are the most beautiful woman I've ever seen. And you look absolutely amazing just the way you are. Come on."

He tugged on my hand and we walked through the crowd. "Where are we going?"

"To a chapel, of course."

Of course.

"You know where one is?"

"It's Vegas. They're everywhere. Let's just stop at the first one we find and get married there."

Caught up in the moment, I laughed. "Deal."

Of course, that deal sounded great in theory. It wasn't until we walked into the Little Chapel of Horrors that featured gothic theme weddings that we both decided maybe it didn't have to be the *first* chapel that we got married in. In fact, the first three chapels we walked into weren't right. Not for us anyway. Ironically, it was the Love Me Tender Chapel, complete with Elvis as the officiant, that we finally settled on. It wasn't fancy. In fact, the building could best be described as cute and maybe even a little retro with the red velvet cushions that lined the pews. It was tucked away, just off the Strip. A small building, badly in need of a coat of paint. It was cheesy and cliché and everything Vegas.

"This one?" Leo looked at me. His eyes danced with laughter.

"I don't think there's another that would be more perfect."

"What can I sign you two up for?" A woman who might very well have been the oldest woman I'd ever laid eyes on appeared from the back room. A cigarette dangled from her lips, and she shuffled painfully slowly down the aisle toward us. "You look like a True Love package couple." She hacked a phlegmy cough and took another pull on her cigarette before she continued.

"True Love package?" I smiled and clutched Leo's hand. It was definitely true love. It had always been true love with us. "I think that—"

"Or...maybe the Cherish the Moment package." The woman eyed us up and down. Leo and I froze, letting her assess us. It felt like the right thing to do. Her eyes landed on me. "Yup. Definitely a Cherish the Moment package."

She turned her back to us and shuffled back down the aisle. Leo and I glanced at each other, but he only shrugged and started to laugh, so it was me who stopped her.

"So," I said a little cautiously, and glanced back to Leo. "What do we do now?"

The woman turned, took the cigarette from her mouth and exhaled in a cloud. "Honey, now you get married." She grinned, a toothless, gaping grin that was both endearing and slightly scary at the same time. "Come with me. I'll get you ready." She pointed her cigarette, the ash dangling dangerously off the tip, at Leo. "You'll go with Burt. Burt!" She hollered out in no general direction. The effort of hollering caused another coughing fit to start deep in her lungs. I wasn't sure whether I should go slap her on the back or find her a glass of water, but before I could make up my mind either way, an overweight elderly man dressed in a white Elvis suit emerged from the back room and made his way only moderately faster down the aisle than his female counterpart had.

"Edna, what's all the hollering about?" He slapped her on the back and then rubbed his palm in a soothing circle where he'd just hit. The action was both aggressive and sweet, and despite the harsh tone he addressed her with, it was easy to see the love between them. I looked up at Leo, who watched the scene with the same look on his face that I must have had. I nodded and smiled. Yes, these two were perfect.

"These kids are ready to tie the knot." Edna waved her hand in our direction and took another drag of her cigarette. "Take the boy and get him ready."

"Kids? Boy?" Leo mouthed the words, and I could tell he was seconds away from bursting into laughter.

Burt straightened and looked us up and down the same way his wife had done. "Cherish the Moment package, huh?"

Edna nodded and hooked her finger at me. "Come on then. We don't have all night. Let's get you hitched."

A shot of nerves flew through my stomach, and as if he sensed it—or maybe he felt it, too—Leo squeezed my hand before he lifted it to his lips and pressed a kiss there. "I'll see you soon." I blinked back sudden and totally ridiculous tears and nodded. It was all I could manage. "I love you, Lex."

"Come on, come on," Edna croaked.

I stood on my tiptoes and gave him a quick kiss on the lips before I released Leo's hand and followed Edna down the aisle into a back room.

THE ROOM WAS jam-packed with everything one would ever need to get married. Silk flower arrangements in an array of colors and designs, many dating back at least thirty years, filled one whole shelf. There was even a rack of dresses and what appeared to be costumes. "You'll need a dress." Edna rifled through the rack and pulled out a yellow floor-length frock that looked like it might have been the height of fashion for a prom dress—in 1973. "This is about your size. It'll hide the—"

"I'm good. What I'm wearing will be just fine."

She gave me a once-over and pursed her lips together. "If you're sure." She crammed the dress back onto the rack. "Your package includes clothes or costumes. Maybe you'd prefer to go with a theme wedding. We have jungle, disco, show girl—"

"I'm good." I smiled and wrapped my arms around my waist. "But what else does the package cover? And what exactly is the Cherish the Moment package?"

Edna pressed her cigarette into a nearby ashtray. "It's the package we give to all our expecting brides." She pulled a fresh smoke out of the package but I couldn't focus on the fact that she shouldn't be smoking so close to me because my brain was still desperately trying to process what she'd just said. "It's the all-inclusive, get it done package."

"Get it done?" I repeated numbly.

"When's the little one due?"

"Pardon?" It was my turn to choke. It took me a few minutes to regulate my breathing and recompose myself, but as soon as I did, I stared openmouthed at the woman who didn't look remotely fazed by the bombshell she'd just dropped on me.

Edna nodded and coughed, but notably didn't light the cigarette between her lips. "Typically the bride wants to get married as quickly as possible, mostly before the groom finds out. Unless your man...nah. He doesn't know anything."

I shook my head, trying to process the fact that she was more or less calling me a sneaky, conniving man trapper as well as the fact that this woman knew within five minutes of meeting me that I was pregnant. "He does...I mean...wait. How did you know?" My hands flew to my stomach and the life, as fragile as it was, that was nestled in there. I'd managed to not obsess about it, or think about how the pregnancy would play out, for at least the last few hours. But within seconds, all of those fears flew back. My lighthearted mood—gone.

"Honey, it's written all over you. Anyone who's looking can see it." She reached over to the shelf beside her and grabbed an oversized bouquet. "And your man, he's obviously not looking. Here." She thrust the bouquet at me. "This will cover the bump."

I looked down at my stomach, which besides being a little thicker than it had been a few years ago, looked exactly the same. I was definitely not showing yet. Or was I?

"I...I don't...I...Maybe this isn't the best idea."

"To get married before he knows about the babe?" She shrugged. "To each their own, but let me tell you, I've been part of hundreds, maybe thousands of weddings, a good deal of them women just like you. It don't make any difference at all if you tell him now or later; point is he made a babe with you and he needs to take responsibility for it. As the mama, you gotta do what's best."

"It's not like that with Leo. We already have a child and..." I drifted off. I wasn't about to stand here and explain myself to this woman when I didn't owe her any type of explanation at all.

No. I didn't owe *her* any explanation. But there was someone I did owe one to.

"I can't do this." I pushed the flower bouquet back onto the shelf. "I can't do this. Not like this."

"We have other packages," Edna rasped. "If you don't want the dress, we can downgrade you to the Happily Ever After package, but you won't get the DVD of pictures. It's not a bad—"

"No." I needed to get out of there. The stale air, suddenly stifling me, threatened to overwhelm me. "I can't do this. I can't do any of this."

~Leo~

BURT WANTED to put me in an Elvis suit, or some other kind of polyester leisure suit thing. He insisted it was "part of the package" but I was able to convince him that what I was wearing was just fine and the chapel probably couldn't handle more than one Elvis. He thrust a box of rings into my hand and told me to pick one of the thin tin bands.

Of course I'd need a ring to put on Lexi's finger. Even if it was a cheap band that would likely turn her finger green. I needed something and I could always upgrade it later. With a diamond. A twinge of guilt that was becoming all too familiar flashed through me. I wouldn't have any money for a diamond. At least not for a while. Not with the hotel. But I couldn't think about that right now. Not moments away from my wedding. Of course, I probably shouldn't be starting our marriage with such a big secret either. Or any secret at all, for that matter.

Dammit.

I slipped a ring from the box and rolled it around my fingers. In only a few minutes, I'd be putting it on the love of my life, forever tying her to me. Finally. For better or for worse, right? Even if *worst* meant investing your entire savings into a hotel without telling your new spouse?

"Shit," I mumbled. I needed to tell her. I couldn't keep it from her any longer than—

"Ready or not, here comes your little lady." Burt cleared his throat with a wet cough that jarred me back to the moment. I wrapped my hand reflexively around the ring and turned around as Burt said, "Don't have the music ready yet. She's not supposed to be—"

"Leo!"

Something was wrong. Lexi wasn't marching or walking or parading down the aisle in any of the ways I imagined she should be. Instead, she was half walking, half running, and the look on her face looked anything but peaceful or as blissful the way a bride should look.

"Leo." Her eyes danced wildly around the room, finally coming to a rest on me. I focused on her and tried to calm her with my gaze as she made her way down the aisle to me in pretty much the most opposite way of what I expected.

"Lexi." I tried to keep my voice even and calm. Whatever was going on, we could manage it. "What's going on? Are you—"

"I can't marry you."

My heart stopped for a beat. "Wait? What?" She finally reached me and I pulled her close, needing to feel her body against mine. "What are you talking about? Of course you can marry me."

She shook her head against my chest and I could feel my shirt grow damp. Dammit, she was crying. *What the hell was going on?* What had happened in the last few minutes to—did she know about the hotel? The money? I stiffened, but forced myself to relax. There was no way.

She pulled back just enough for me to see her face and the tears in her eyes. The sadness I saw there almost broke me. This wasn't supposed to be happening. Everything had been perfect. Well, almost perfect.

"Leo, I have to tell...I..."

"What? You have to tell me what?"

Confusion crossed her face and for a split second, I thought I saw something else there. Fear? But then it was gone.

"Do you want me to start the music?" Burt started to mutter and shuffle around behind us. "Edna! Start the music."

"No." I turned and held up a hand to stop him. "Just give us a minute." I turned back to Lexi. "What's going on? What do you need to tell me?"

"Leo, I—"

She was cut off when the speakers crackled to life. It wasn't the wedding march, but what sounded like the music for "Love Me Tender." Sure enough, Burt's gravelly voice joined in with the music and Lexi and I both turned to stare at the old man in his full Elvis regalia, belting out what was no doubt supposed to be a romantic tune. There was nothing left to do but shake my head. Next to me, I could feel Lexi start to shake. I wrapped my arm around her and pulled her close before I realized she wasn't crying but laughing. Well, it was a mixture of tears and laughter. Either way, I looked down at her face as she bit her lip trying, and failing, to contain her hysterical giggles. Her hand flew up to her mouth as a sound that was half laugh, half sob escaped.

"Come on." I wrapped my hand around hers. "Let's get out of here."

CHAPTER SEVEN

~Lexi~

Sitting by the pool, letting the sun warm my legs, I couldn't help but let myself actually enjoy Vegas. Nicole was probably right. Las Vegas wasn't all bad. Maybe I'd even tell her that. I glanced at my cell phone and the unanswered texts she'd sent me already that morning. I had no real reason for ignoring her, except I knew she wanted details on our trip and I wasn't sure I had any to give her.

Especially after my little breakdown the night before in the chapel. After Leo pulled me outside, we'd laughed until I started to cry again and then I couldn't be sure whether I was crying because of the secret I was keeping or because the whole situation had been so ludicrous. All I knew was that I needed to get out of there. I'd given Leo some excuse about wanting Ben with us, which wasn't an excuse at all. There was no real way we could have gotten married without our son, and we both knew it.

He'd looked relieved, as if he hadn't wanted to go through with it either, and now in the light of a new day, that was the thing that was bothering me the most. The look on his face when I'd told him I couldn't marry him was definitely one of relief.

Why?

We needed to talk, that much was clear, but I'd slept in and when I finally got out of bed there was a note on the pillow that he'd taken Ben and gone to try out the paddle boards, so I'd slipped out to the pool to enjoy a tea in the morning sun.

Over the pool in the distance, I could see figures out in the middle of the lake. I wasn't worried about either of them because they were both confident swimmers. Ben was happiest when he could be in, on, or around water and after a few years living at the lake, Leo had become just as comfortable with the water. Besides, I knew Leo wouldn't take any chances with Ben.

I took a quick glance around, looking for what, I wasn't sure. There was nobody around considering the hotel wasn't really open, but still, I hadn't been comfortable in a bathing suit in years, not since the miscarriages started and my once flat stomach started to store a little extra padding. My hand slid between the folds of my robe and rested on my stomach where there was a little life starting to grow and develop. Was it possible my belly was already growing?

I said a silent prayer that the little sprout was still okay before I slipped off the robe altogether and padded over to the pool's edge. I didn't have any goggles or a swim cap because it had been so long since I'd been in a pool, but it didn't matter. The water was like a magnet that pulled me toward it.

I lifted my arms over my head. My body remembered what it was supposed to do as I pushed up off the concrete and arced up into a perfect dive. The water sluiced over me, cocooning and cleansing me all at the same time. I kicked hard, staying

under as long as I could in a streamline position. But it had been
so long since I'd been in the pool, my lungs didn't have nearly
the capacity as they used to and I surfaced before I wanted to,
with a gasp. I didn't let that deter me, and with a hard kick, I
launched my right arm out of the water and pulled, propelling
me forward. My muscles strained and protested but a thrill ran
through my body at the exertion. It felt good to swim again.
Really good.

My body fell easily into the rhythm and when I approached
the cement wall at the far end, without even thinking about it, I
tucked into a flip turn and pushed easily off the wall and back
into a streamline. I didn't bother counting the laps, but instead
allowed my mind to wander. I'd always used swimming as a way
to decompress, think through things that were bothering me or
needed an answer that I couldn't seem to come to any other
way. It had always been the ultimate stress relief, so why had it
been so long since I'd allowed myself the luxury of a swim?

The answer was easy. Life got in the way and my own needs
had been pushed aside. That and the swimming season in a
Canadian glacier-fed lake was considerably shorter than a pool
in Nevada. I laughed a little; bubbles slipped out of my mouth
as I reached the edge of the wall for my final lap. The sun
warmed my head the moment I surfaced and I ran my hands
through my hair, wringing out the extra water.

"Impressive."

The voice jolted me and I had a flash of déjà vu from years
ago, with Leo staring down at me in the glare of the sun of the
MGM hotel on the Strip. But it wasn't Leo who looked down at
me this time, but Roxanne, Keith's girlfriend.

"Sorry," she said. "I didn't mean to startle you."

"You didn't," I lied, but put a bright smile on my face. "And
it's hardly impressive. I can't remember the last time I swam
laps." I pulled myself up onto the edge of the pool and accepted

the towel she handed me. I wrapped it quickly around my waist without bothering to dry myself at all.

"Well, you sure looked good out there," Roxanne said. We walked back to where I'd left my robe on the chair and sat side by side. "I can't even swim. Well, not in any way that counts. Mostly I just splash around with the kids or float with a drink in my hand." She laughed and I found myself instantly liking her. We hadn't had much of a chance to chat except for dinner the first night, and that had been a loud, busy night full of kids and the usual getting to know each other stuff. Despite our limited contact, my first impression of her had been of a quiet woman who seemed a little unsure of herself. Which had seemed a bit strange to me considering Keith was so outgoing and smooth. Pretty much the epitome of a Las Vegas event planner and hotel manager. But maybe that's why they worked.

"Well, floating around with a drink sounds like a pretty good use of the pool, too." I felt like a fraud as I spoke the words when there was no way I'd be having a drink any time soon. Well, hopefully not anyway. But I couldn't tell her that.

"We'll have to do that later this afternoon while the guys are working."

"Working?" I still hadn't had a chance to talk to Leo about what Keith said about investing in Oasis. There was no way we could do it. For so many reasons. Not the least of which was the money factor. It was too much money and as much as I knew Leo would love the challenge to turn the resort around and make it into something great, there was just no way we could uproot Ben and sink all our money into it. There was just no way.

"Of course." Roxanne twisted her long, dark hair around her fingers before she tossed it all over her shoulder. "Now that the investors are all on board, they can really get to work and hopefully have everything in place for a soft opening at Christmas."

She spoke so fast I almost didn't catch it, but my brain twigged onto the one phrase I knew meant everything was about to be different. "What do you mean, 'now that the investors are all on board'?"

I knew the answer to the question before she opened her mouth and by the look on her face, she realized too late that she'd said too much.

"Well," she continued cautiously. "Now that Leo has committed to being the final investor, they can get—"

"Leo's *committed*?" The words came out of my mouth, and they tasted sour on my tongue. "How could he...but he didn't..." We hadn't talked about anything. In fact, he hadn't even mentioned the opportunity to me. Keith had. Was he trying to keep it from me? How could he, though? Moving our family from Canada back to Las Vegas was, well...it was huge. He couldn't make that decision on his own. My brain spun; too many scenarios and thoughts slammed through me. I couldn't keep up with the twisted mess flying through my head. Was the hotel project something he wanted to do on his own? Maybe he didn't want us to come. Was he... "Oh God, I think I'm going to be sick."

I managed to run to the bushes only moments before I emptied the meager contents of my stomach into them. I felt rather than heard Roxanne come to stand behind me. She slid her hand up and down my back while I wiped my face. "Lexi, I'm so sorry. I thought you knew. Are you okay? Can I get you anything?"

I waited until I was sure I wouldn't be sick again before I slowly stood up. I nodded in reaction to her questions, but didn't make eye contact with her. I couldn't. I didn't want to see the look in her eyes. That look that said, *I'm sorry your husband lied to you.* But he wasn't my husband. Technically, he didn't have any legal responsibility to me at all, only Ben. Is that what this was all about? He wanted to leave? He wasn't in love with me anymore?

I knew my mind was going to places it shouldn't. I knew I was being irrational and ridiculous, but still I couldn't seem to stop myself.

"Lexi?" Roxanne bent down so I had no choice but to look her in the eyes. "Are you okay? Do you normally get sick like that when you...well, I've never seen someone throw up like that before. Except for myself, of course, but that's when I was pregnant with Ruby and then I swear I couldn't keep anything down. Especially if anyone told me anything that was remotely stressful, I'd—" She clapped a hand over her mouth and her eyes got wide.

"It's not what you—"

"Oh my God, are you—"

We spoke at the same time. But I recovered first and made a split-second decision to go with direct honesty. "Roxanne," I said softly, imploring her with my eyes. "Please don't say anything, okay?"

"To Ben?" She shook her head. "Of course not. I wouldn't—"

"To Leo." I swallowed hard. "And of course, not to Keith."

"Leo doesn't know?" Confusion clouded her eyes and she glanced behind her, as if the men would be hovering. "How can he not...how far along are you?"

Both were questions I didn't want to answer, but I could tell she wasn't going to be satisfied until I said something. "It's just not a good time to worry him with it right now."

"Why would he be worried about a baby?"

Tears welled up in my eyes and I couldn't answer her because there was no answer for that question. Besides, from what she'd just told me, it wasn't Leo who should be worried about the truth. It was me.

~Leo~

"THIS IS the coolest thing I've ever done."

I looked over at Ben, who was balanced like a pro on his board, paddling through the water with an ease that made me more than a little bit jealous as my toes dug into the foam under my feet in a desperate attempt to keep my balance.

"Dad, hurry up and catch up to me," Ben called moments before he dug his paddle in and moved even farther away.

"I would if you stopped moving long enough," I yelled after him. The action caused me to lose what little balance I had. I dropped to my knees to keep from plunging into the water and making a fool of myself, again. "This is fucking stupid," I muttered under my breath.

"I heard that." Ben laughed and circled around closer to me. "Mom said using curse words is the sign of low intelligence."

"Your mother is right." I slowly stood again and took a moment to find my center of gravity again. "But sometimes the only word to fit a situation is a curse word. But only if you're an adult," I added quickly. I could only imagine what Lexi would say if that piece of information found its way back to her. "So don't try it."

Ben laughed again and brought his board to a stop next to mine. "You need to relax, Dad. You're trying too hard. That's why you keep falling."

"That doesn't make any sense." I tensed my body and reached forward with the paddle, wobbling uncontrollably. "How am I supposed to relax?"

"Just breathe. It's just like standing on the ground. There's no reason you would fall over standing on the beach, right? So don't fall over on the board."

He made it sound so simple, too simple. I snuck a glance at him and quickly looked away again because it was only discouraging to see the way he ran up and down, with no concern for balance, or falling into the cold water. "Seriously, Dad. Breathe."

I did as instructed, because I had nothing to lose by trying. I closed my eyes, inhaled deeply and filled my lungs before I exhaled slowly. I did it two more times before I reached forward with my paddle and dipped it into the water. To my surprise, the board moved easily through the water and even better, I didn't wobble at all.

"See? It works."

I opened my eyes slowly and saw him in my peripheral, moving slowly alongside me. "It does seem to be working," I admitted reluctantly.

"Just keep breathing, Dad."

I did as my son suggested and it worked. After a few minutes, I relaxed my toes and even started to enjoy myself. We paddled around the bay in front of the hotel's beach, and at one point I was even comfortable enough to risk a glance at Oasis. There was no doubt it could be a beautiful resort with a little bit of work. Work I was more than willing to put in. But first, I had a few minor—okay...not so minor—details to work out.

"So what do you think of it here?" I asked the question casually as we pulled the boards up onto the beach and flipped them upside-down. "Do you like it? Think you could see yourself spending a little time here?"

"Of course." Ben grabbed my paddle and took them to the storage shed next to the board rack. "This is the coolest place ever," he said when he returned. "I'd love to hang out here more often and Evan and Ruby are awesome. Can they come visit us at home? After we're back? I think they'd like our lake, too. But it's probably too cold for them. They're such wusses—they think *this* lake is too cold." Ben laughed and I gave him a minute before trying to pull him back to the conversation at hand.

"So, if I was to talk to your mom about maybe having a change of scenery for a while, do you think you'd be okay with that or would you miss your friends too much?" I knew it probably wasn't the best way to approach the conversation of potentially moving to Lake Las Vegas, especially considering I still hadn't said anything to Lexi. I hadn't really planned to try to get Ben on board first, but hanging out with him on the water, it just seemed like a good time to ask him about it. Besides, I was pretty sure I knew what he'd say.

"Like *live* here?" His eyes got wide and he stared at me. "Instead of Lake Lillian? What about Mom?"

"Well, of course Mom, too."

"But we live there."

"We could live here."

"Why?"

"Why not?"

He thought about that one for a moment before he shrugged.

"So?" I asked. "What do you think? Would that be something you'd like?"

"Would I get to play on the paddle boards?"

I nodded. "Of course."

He glanced up the beach in the direction of the pools.

"And the pools, too, of course," I added before he could ask.

It took a moment for him to digest what I was saying, but then a smile crept across his face and he nodded. "I think that'd be cool." I slapped him on the back and then spontaneously pulled him into a hug. It wasn't often that he'd let me hug him these days. He was getting too cool and maybe just a little too old to be giving hugs to his old man. "What did Mom say?" he asked, his face lined with concern, when I released him.

He was a smart kid and no doubt he knew exactly what his mom would say, or possibly had already said.

"Well...I still need to talk to her about it."

"Ah, man! I knew it." Ben kicked his foot into the sand, hard. And turned away. "Mom's never going to go for it. She hates it here."

"I don't think that's true." I caught up to him as he made his way up the beach. "In fact, we had a really fun night last night." There was no point mentioning the near wedding and the subsequent tears. "Actually, that's something else I wanted to talk to you about."

Ben stopped and looked at me. I gestured to a bench nearby. I wanted to talk to Ben alone before I saw Lexi and even though the resort was big, I had a feeling it wasn't big enough.

He sat and stared at me, no doubt waiting for some bad news. I wasn't sure how'd he react to what I was about to ask, but just like with the last big question, I had my suspicions. "So I've been thinking," I began slowly. "The other day you were talking about how some of the kids bug you that your mom and I aren't married."

He narrowed his eyes and tilted his head so I continued.

"Well, maybe it's about time we fixed that. What do you think?"

Ben bit his bottom lip and took his time before he answered. "But if we move here, then I don't have to worry about those kids any more, right?"

I hadn't anticipated that. "True. But there might be other kids," I suggested. "Besides, I think it might be a nice thing for your mom and me to do, don't you? A nice dress, some flowers, a cake."

"Cake?"

Boys really were too easy. "Yes." I tried not to laugh. "There's usually cake at weddings."

His smile was wide and split his face. "Then I think she'd probably like that."

I did laugh then. "I think so, too. You know what I think she'd like even more?"

He shook his head.

"If you would be my best man." It was an idea I'd mentioned casually that night Ben told us about his troubles at school, and after our near wedding, one that had become much clearer in my head. Maybe a cheesy Elvis wedding on the Strip with two chain smokers for witnesses wasn't the perfect way to get married, but one thing our near-miss nuptials had shown me was that I did want to marry Lexi. More than anything. And I couldn't think of a better way to do it than with Ben at my side. He should have been there from the start. There was no way I could get married without my little man by my side.

"Really?"

The look on his face was priceless. A mixture of shock and joy. Perfect. "Of course."

He let out a whoop and fist pumped the air. "This is so much better than being a stupid ring bearer." I laughed, remembering when Lexi told me how disappointed Ben had been when he hadn't been able to be the ring bearer in Nicole and Ryan's wedding five years earlier. And he was right: it was *way* better than being a stupid ring bearer.

"Come on." Ben grabbed my hand and yanked me off the beach.

"Where are we going?" I went along with him, surprised at the strength he had. It was kind of shocking how fast he was becoming an actual man.

"We have to tell Mom. She's going to be so psyched."

"Whoa." I put the brakes on and yanked Ben to a stop. "Hang on a second." I glanced over his shoulder up the hill to where I could see Lexi and Roxanne sitting next to the pool. Over toward the main building, Keith and the kids looked as if they were sitting down to breakfast. I couldn't tell Ben the details of why I didn't want him to run off and tell Lexi the good news, not before I had a chance to talk to her myself. There were too many things we needed to clear up because besides the realization the night before that I wanted more than anything to make her my wife, I also realized that I couldn't live with all the secrets between us. Not since that first major secret after all our years apart, the secret of my son, had we ever kept anything from each other. We'd sworn to be upfront with each other no matter what.

So what had changed?

I shook my head, clearing the question and looked down at Ben, who watched me with a strange expression.

"Why can't we tell Mom?"

I forced a smile and opened my mouth to tell him what I hoped wouldn't turn out to be another lie. "Because even though your mom and I have talked about marriage, I've never actually proposed and I think she deserves a pretty awesome proposal. Don't you?"

His face lit up in a smile, just the way I knew it would. There was no one Ben loved more than his mom, and he loved nothing more than making her happy.

He was a lot like his dad that way.

CHAPTER EIGHT

~Lexi~

Thinking about Leo and the baby and the hotel and pretty much everything that had happened in the last forty-eight hours was making me crazy. I couldn't sit still. I couldn't eat. I couldn't do anything. I'd excused myself from Roxanne, and made up some lame excuse about my stomach being unsettled as to why I wasn't joining everyone for breakfast. It was partially true. It *was* unsettled. Hell, all of me was unsettled.

I'd asked Roxanne to tell Leo I'd gone to lie down, and I'd see him after breakfast. It was absolutely the chicken thing to do. And I knew it. But when I saw him with Ben, talking on the beach after they got in from the paddle boards, my heart just broke a little bit. If Leo was considering moving to Vegas and leaving us behind, Ben would be without a father.

Again.

I'd done that to him once with Andrew, the only father he'd known when he was a little boy.

But that was different. Leo *was* his father. He wouldn't leave Ben. He wouldn't leave me.

Would he?

No. I knew in my heart he wouldn't leave. I was just being hormonal or overtired, or oversensitive, or over something.

What I really needed to do was talk to Leo. I needed to figure out what the real story was with Oasis and everything else. Part of me had been waiting for him to come to me and tell me the truth about what Keith had asked of him. But with every minute that went by, it looked more and more as if that wasn't going to happen. In fact, if what Roxanne said was true, Leo had already made his decisions about everything without talking to me.

No.

I couldn't believe that. This was Leo I was talking about. *My* Leo. He would never keep such a thing from me.

But you're keeping a secret from him.

My stupid inner voice piped up again. I couldn't listen to her—to myself. In search of a distraction, I crossed our suite— our extremely large and well-appointed suite—and opened the bathroom door. The room was so large it was almost as big as the living room of our house back home, and despite the marble floors and oversized tub with an even larger steam shower on the other side of the room, there was something cozy about the bathroom. I would have expected such a room to look ostentatious, or cold, but the color scheme of ivory with brown and gold flecks was almost cozy. And the fireplace, which seemed kind of out of place in the desert, created a sense of warmth that I desperately needed at that moment.

I turned the taps and filled the tub, letting the room fill with steam. There was an assortment of oils and bath salts on the counter. The hotel was well-stocked, despite the barebones staff. Roxanne had explained that Keith had brought in a few key people who would start hiring the rest of the staff and setting the operating procedures for the resort, so even though they weren't officially open, the people they did have were already getting into the groove. And I definitely appreciated it. Especially the decadent bath products that Joanne, the woman who would be in charge of housekeeping, provided. Our little house in Canada didn't have a big bathtub. Heck, it didn't have a bathtub at all and it was definitely one of the luxuries I missed.

I chose a bottle of lavender oil and poured it under the water, watching the bubbles fill the tub before I shed my wet bathing suit and robe in the middle of the floor. I tried to avoid the mirror, the way I did more and more these days. Pregnancy was hard on a body. Multiple miscarriages were very hard. And it wasn't just the extra padding and stretch marks that crossed my abdomen that bothered me. No. It was more than that. My hand cupped the fleshy skin there and rubbed small circles.

It was definitely more than just the physical changes. It was the betrayal of my body that bothered me the most. The fact that time after time it wouldn't allow me to carry the babies we'd conceived out of love. There was no reason the doctors could find for the miscarriages. There was no reason I shouldn't be able to have another baby.

But you might have one now.

That little voice chirped up again. I looked up, so that despite myself, I stared at my naked reflection in the large mirror. Instead of glancing away quickly, I let myself—no, I *made* myself—take it all in and really look at myself for the first time in a long time. Finally, when I was done taking stock, I homed in on my stomach and the life that was contained there.

I did the math in my head. It had been just over thirteen weeks. The longest I'd carried a baby since Ben. It took a moment for the realization to hit me. Thirteen weeks. I looked up so I stared at my own eyes in the mirror.

"Thirteen weeks."

Like the doctor said, that was out of the danger zone. There was a real chance this was going to happen. A *real* chance.

Which meant I had to tell Leo. He'd be thrilled.

Will he?

My conversation with Roxanne ran through my head again. If Leo had already made his decision about staying in Vegas...no. I wasn't going to think about that yet. Not until I talked to Leo.

And I wasn't going to do that until after I had my bath.

I stepped into the water. A sigh escaped my lips as I sank down and let the water surround me. I giggled as I slipped deeper, and the bubbles covered me so I could barely see. I may have gone a little overboard with the bath oils.

I rested my head back against the cool marble and closed my eyes as a smile played on my lips at the knowledge that I was actually pregnant and for the first time since I'd taken the test— maybe even a little hopeful.

~Leo~

"Lexi?"

The bathroom was full of steam and I could hear the bath running. But I couldn't see Lexi. Not that I could see anything through the mist. There was definitely a ventilation problem. I slid my hand along the wall and found the switch that started the fan. I'd left Ben at breakfast when Roxanne told me Lexi wasn't feeling well and had gone to lie down. It didn't sound right. It wasn't like Lexi to leave like that. Not unless she was really sick, and something told me she wasn't. I just hoped she wasn't worked up about the night before. Either way, I wasn't going to sit there and eat eggs Benedict without seeing whether she was okay.

"Lexi?" I called her name again. "Are you in here?" I stepped inside the room and into—water? Panic pricked at the back of my neck. "Lexi!"

The fan had started to clear some of the steam and I ran as best as I could on the slippery floor to the bath, turning off the taps as I reached into the water for Lexi. If something had happened to her.... If she'd done something....

No.

The bath was huge. Almost like a small pool.

Finally, my hands wrapped around her thigh and I squeezed as I yanked on her leg. At that exact moment, the steam cleared enough for me to see her head fly upright from a position of relaxation.

But it was too late.

"What the hell?"

Her eyes flew open, wild and panicked until they landed on mine. Then it was only confusion I saw there.

"Leo? What are you doing?"

I looked her up and down, able to see her clearly now as the steam vanished. She was fine. Probably more than fine. She looked as if she'd been enjoying a bath.

"You didn't answer," I said lamely. "I couldn't see you...and the water...there was water."

"What are you talking about?" She pushed back so she sat up, her arms wrapped over her naked breasts. A fact I was more than a little disappointed in.

I gestured to the water I was currently kneeling in and her hand flew up to her mouth, leaving one breast momentarily exposed. "Oh my God. I must have fallen asleep. It was so warm and I was so…" Her words dissolved into a giggle.

I couldn't help it; I started to laugh as well as the panic I'd felt only moments earlier evaporated. I moved up so I could sit on the ledge of the marble tub, which afforded me a much better view of her nakedness. A view my body appreciated in all the ways that mattered. And all the ways that made me want to get into that tub with her. The only thing that stopped me was the knowledge that she hadn't been feeling well.

"Are you okay?" I asked her once the laughter had dried up. "Roxanne said you needed to lie down. That you weren't feeling very good."

Her face changed in an instant. All traces of humor were gone. "I'm fine, Leo. I just needed a few minutes by myself and I wasn't very hungry, so I thought I should…you know what?" She changed tack so suddenly that it took me a moment to catch up. "I think we need to talk."

I nodded. We did need to talk. I hated that there was any secret between us and she must have felt it, too. The fact that I might have caused her any uncertainty or unhappiness by keeping things to myself made me sick. From the moment I'd met Lexi, I'd done nothing but love her. Even through all the years we'd been apart, I'd always loved her and the last thing I'd ever wanted to do was hurt her. I fetched an oversized plush towel from the rack and held it out for her.

She stood in the bath, hot water dripping off her body. For the first time in longer than I could remember, she didn't try to cover herself, or turn away so I couldn't see her nakedness. Instead, her eyes locked on mine and she held my gaze, almost challenging me to look my fill.

So I did.

I started at her gorgeous face—just as stunning as the day I'd met her—and traveled down her smooth, long neck. There was a familiar tug in my groin as my gaze traveled down the swell of her chest to each perfect, full breast. I inhaled a shaky breath, trying to control the urge to reach for her as I let my eyes travel to her stomach and the swell of her belly, down to the apex of where her thighs—

Wait.

The swell of her belly?

My eyes stopped their downward descent and flew back up to her abdomen and then farther up, to Lexi's eyes. A smile danced across her face as she realized I'd noticed a change. A change that was definitely different than the last time I'd laid eyes on her.

I tipped my head in question, not able to voice the question I so desperately wanted to ask. "Lexi?" I finally managed. "Is...what..."

I couldn't finish my thought but that was okay because Lexi simply nodded in response. And it was all I needed. The second she stepped out of the tub and onto the floor, I jumped up and pulled her into me tight. Her towel fell away; her wet, naked skin pressed against my clothes, dampening them, and nothing had ever felt more right.

My hands cupped her face to tilt her head slightly as I pressed my lips to hers. I planned on kissing her gently, sweetly, but the second I got a taste of her, my instincts kicked in and all I wanted to do was claim her and the baby in her belly as mine.

Somehow, I held myself back, restraining myself from taking all that I wanted. I would never do anything out of selfish need that would put Lexi and this baby in danger. But I would tell her and more importantly, show her just how amazingly beautiful she was. I moved my mouth down to her bare shoulder, leaving a trail of kisses on her soft skin while I inhaled the sweet scent of lavender that clung to her from her bath.

I half expected her to push me away, to reach for her towel

and cover her luscious body but when a moan escaped her lips, I knew she wouldn't.

"You are so gorgeous, Lexi."

"No, I—"

"Are more beautiful than the day I met you." My eyes locked on hers and I held them until I could see it in her that she believed what I said. I let my hands slide down her body, just tracing the swell of her breasts before they gently cupped her tummy and the life she grew inside. I held my breath before I asked the question I both dreaded the answer to and wanted to know more than anything. Of course I was excited about the baby. More than excited. But I was also cautious. Hesitant because of the losses we'd already suffered. Each one broke me more than the last and I knew the pain I went through was nothing compared to the total devastation Lexi felt every time the bleeding started.

My hand rubbed a small circle on the bump that seemed bigger than any of the others. In fact, I couldn't remember seeing a bump before at all. No indication that there was life inside before it was gone. I could never decide what was worse. Finally, I found the courage to ask, "How long?"

Her mouth twitched up in a small smile before it disappeared.

I didn't want to get my hopes up. I couldn't. But when she said, "Thirteen weeks," my brain did the quick calculation. Just over three months. Longer than any other pregnancy we'd had. Much longer. Long enough that...maybe...

"Thirteen?"

She nodded.

"So...it's..."

Lexi shrugged. "I hope so. When I saw the doctor, she—"

"You already saw the doctor?"

She nodded. "About a week ago."

"And you didn't tell me?"

"I didn't want to worry you."

Something that wasn't quite anger, but wasn't too far off either, rose inside me. How could she keep something like this from me? How could she possibly think that I wouldn't want to know about a baby? *Our* baby.

"Lexi..." My hands clenched into fists at my sides and I turned away. I needed space. I needed to breathe so I didn't get upset with her, but—damn. I couldn't wrap my brain around it. "Worry me?" I asked the question without looking at her. I knew what I'd see on her face anyway. I'd see hurt, pain, confusion. All the things I was feeling, too.

"Yes," she said. I could hear her move, likely wrapping the towel around her body again, closing herself off to me. "Every time this happens, it ends badly. I didn't want you to...I couldn't..."

"What?" I turned and saw the tears in her eyes. "What didn't you want?"

Her voice was soft, barely a whisper when she said, "I couldn't stand to see you disappointed again when it didn't work out."

I closed the gap between us and held her tight, needing to feel the closeness between us when there was clearly so much distance. I couldn't stand it. I needed her close. I needed her to understand that there should only ever be closeness between us. "Lexi." I nuzzled into her hair and inhaled the essence of the woman I loved. "There should never be secrets between us. We need to tell each other everything." She stiffened in my arms and I knew instantly I'd made a mistake.

She pulled slowly out of my grasp. "You're right, Leo." Her eyes were dark and hard as she assessed me. "There shouldn't be secrets between us. So why don't you tell me exactly what you've been keeping from me?"

~Lexi~

IT WASN'T AT ALL how I'd wanted to tell Leo about the baby and I definitely hadn't wanted to confront him about Oasis the way I had, but sometimes things just worked out in ways you didn't expect and ultimately, it was a good thing. We needed to get everything out in the open and say what needed to be said. Although, the look on his face almost broke me. Something deep inside hurt to know that there was something that might be broken between us. Something that never should have been allowed to break. But now that I'd said what I needed to say, I couldn't go back. Nor should I.

"Tell me the truth, Leo." I softened my eyes and searched his face for the truth I needed to see there. "Tell me what's going on with this place. What did you do?"

His head dropped momentarily before he stood tall again. "Lexi, I didn't mean for it to happen the way it did. Of course you know I would never make any decisions about our life without talking to you first."

I'd thought I'd known that and even though it should have, hearing the words from his lips didn't reassure me the way I would have thought. Everything Roxanne had told me echoed in my head and everything I'd been feeling all morning crashed down again. Was it *our* life he'd been making decisions for, or *his*? I reached for his hand, needing to connect with him somehow. "Talk to me, Leo."

Not knowing what he was hiding from me was killing me. It was exhausting trying to be patient, when that was the very last thing I wanted to do.

"Lexi." He looked down at his feet and wouldn't meet my eyes. That's all I needed to know to understand that I wasn't going to like what he told me. Yes, I'd kept a secret. But not one that would hurt him and I knew without a doubt that whatever he was about to say was definitely going to hurt me.

My protective instincts took over and I squeezed my eyes shut. Maybe if I couldn't see him, whatever it was that he was going to tell me wouldn't be so bad.

"The last thing I want to do is hurt you, Lexi."

Like a toddler trying to ignore something that they didn't want to deal with, I shook my head but still wouldn't open my eyes.

"Lexi." He squeezed my hand. "I was never trying to—"

"If you want to leave I won't stop you."

"Wait, what?" I still wouldn't look at him. "Lexi, look at me." His fingers latched around my upper arm and he squeezed just hard enough for me to finally look at him. The expression in his eyes was wild. I'd seen every emotion on Leo's face from sadness to joy and everything in between, but I'd never seen him look at me the way he looked at me at that moment. "What are you talking about?" He spoke so softly, I almost didn't hear him. "Leave you?"

Tears sprang to my eyes as I heard him speak the words I didn't even want to think about.

"Talk to me," he urged. "Please."

"Roxanne told me about the hotel," I admitted. "That Keith wanted you as an investor." I took a breath and exhaled slowly before I added, "And that you said yes."

Leo's face dropped as the realization of what I was saying sank in. "And so you thought I wanted to do this." He waved his hands, encompassing the bathroom, but mostly what lay beyond it. "You thought I wanted to do this...by myself?"

I nodded.

"Lexi." His hands dropped away from my arms, leaving me

feeling strangely empty. "Why would you...how could you? I just don't understand."

Suddenly cold, I crossed my arms around my waist, hugging myself and our unborn baby. "Is it true?"

"Is what true?"

"Did you agree to invest in the Oasis?"

He pressed his lips together and nodded once.

I had to swallow hard to keep myself from crying. "Then how could I not think that, Leo?" The urge to cry pressed hard against my throat. "You made a huge decision. A life-changing decision. And you didn't even talk to me. What else could I think?" My arms shook. I clung harder to myself in an effort to maintain control.

"You could not think that I was going to leave you." He spun on his heel and paced away from me in the cavernous bathroom. Just when I thought he was going to leave the room, he spun around hard and stared at me. "God, Lexi. You could give me the benefit of the doubt. After everything we've been through. Everything we've done together. Our life. Ben." I swallowed hard when he said our son's name. "You really think that I'd just leave?" There was so much pain and hurt in his eyes that I could no longer hold in the tears. They slid unchecked down my cheeks. He shook his head and looked away, an action that hurt me more than anything else he could have said.

But it angered me, too. His response to this entire conversation angered me. Of course I could think that. What reason had he given me lately that would allow me any other way of thinking? I crossed the tile floor and retrieved the robe that hung on the wall, tying the plush material around my body before I turned back to him. He hadn't moved and the break had given me a chance to compose myself. "What else could I think, Leo?"

He opened his mouth to speak, but I didn't give him a

chance. "You brought us down here without telling me what it was really about. You kept it from me. A decision that affects both of us and you didn't think it was important to mention it. And then you accepted Keith's offer." I swallowed hard at that and what it really meant. "An offer that definitely involves us both and pretty much every penny we have. No." I waved my hand wildly before I tucked it into the pocket of the robe. "It involves *every* penny we have. And some we don't. Two hundred and fifty thousand dollars, Leo? Really? What were you thinking? We don't even have that kind of money. Not unless—"

I couldn't finish my thought because at that moment I realized just how he had found the money to buy into the Oasis and it didn't include the inheritance from Uncle Ray the way I'd originally thought. No. It was... "The inn." It wasn't a question, but he still nodded in response.

"How could you...the inn? You love the inn. You turned it around, made it successful, made it...yours."

"I can't run them both, Lex. I—"

"You did this. You made this decision without so much as a word to me about it." Hurt and pain flowed through me. From the moment we'd arrived in Vegas, I'd known something was up. Heck, I knew it before we'd even left. But I'd become really good at ignoring things I didn't want to deal with, and that's exactly what I'd been doing. Even after talking to Keith and Roxanne, part of me thought—no, hoped—that Leo would tell me it wasn't true. I'd never felt so gutted, so completely stripped open. I couldn't stand there anymore. I couldn't look at him. Not knowing that he would do such a thing. I had to get out.

I moved as carefully as I could with the slippery floor beneath my feet toward the bedroom carpet.

"Lexi." Leo's hand grabbed for my arm and I both spun and slipped in his grasp. Fear shot through me as I started to fall but in a flash, his arms surrounded me and pulled me tight to him, both safe from the fall and in danger of having my heart broken further. "Are you okay? I didn't mean to...God, babe, if anything..." He nuzzled his face into my hair and breathed deeply; his arms tightened their grip on me.

The tears continued to flow down my face. How could I love this man so much and be so completely shattered by him and his actions at the same time?

"You have to know I'd never do anything to hurt you." I could hear the pain in his voice. "I love you and Ben more than anything in the world. I'd never do anything to...I should have told you."

I nodded against his chest.

"I didn't know how to bring it up. I know how much you love it at the lake and to be honest, I didn't have any intention of even entertaining Keith's offer." I wiggled in his grip just enough so I could look at him while he spoke. I needed to see the truth in his eyes, and it was there. "Originally I thought coming here would be a good chance to get away," he continued. "To have a bit of a break before the holiday season. I know how hard you've been working and Ben's troubles at school this year with the other kids. We've all been so busy, we needed a bit of a family holiday."

I couldn't argue with that.

"But when I got here and..."

"Saw the potential?" I finished for him. I knew Leo well enough to know exactly how his brain would have kicked into high gear when he saw the opportunity that Oasis represented, and the idea of a project he could really sink his teeth into. His dark eyes flashed and he nodded.

"It's incredible."

I nodded. "It is." And I knew in that moment, that even though I hated how he'd gone about it and I couldn't agree with the fact that he'd made the decision without me, I *could* agree with the actual decision. I'd never known anyone the way I knew Leo and I'd known from the moment I set foot outside the limo at the Oasis that the resort was his future.

But so were we. Myself, Ben, and...the baby.

How could he have it all?

CHAPTER NINE

~Leo~

I stroked Lexi's hair, her head in my lap as she drifted off to sleep. It was still early in the day, and Lexi rarely napped, but it wasn't every day we had emotionally draining conversations. And it was definitely not every day that she was carrying a baby. Our baby. My hand snuck down to her abdomen and I floated my hand over her skin, careful not to wake her. I still couldn't get over the fact that she was so far along and I was just finding out. Logically I knew why she'd kept it a secret. Hell, from the sound of it, she'd denied it to herself for weeks...months, too. I got it. I really did.

But thirteen weeks?

That changed everything. I knew I shouldn't let myself get my hopes up too much, but I couldn't help it. I had a good feeling about this time. Scratch that, I had a good feeling about *everything*. I'd screwed up by not talking to Lexi about the hotel. I'd screwed up big time and for a moment I thought maybe it was too much, but one thing I knew was never to underestimate my love.

We'd talked and she saw the potential in Oasis just as I had. We still needed to talk to Ben, but at least now we were both on the same page and as long as he didn't have any strong objections about staying in Las Vegas for a little bit—which, given our conversation earlier, I doubted—we'd give it a try. And now with a baby on the way, it might just be the fresh start we needed as a family.

I bent to press a kiss to Lexi's forehead before I slid out from under her. She needed to sleep, and when she was rested and ready, we'd talk to Ben. Until then, I had a lot to discuss with Keith. Including the financing details for the deal. It was no small amount of money and Lexi had a point: we needed to take a long, hard look at our finances and how we could make it happen.

But first things first. I had one very major thing to take care of. I let the door to our suite close softly behind me and went to find my son to help me out.

He was right where I left him, scarfing down waffles at the breakfast table with Roxanne's two kids. "Are you still eating?" I glanced at the clock on the wall. I'd been gone for over an hour. "Do you have a hollow leg?"

"No." He looked at me as if I'd just sprouted a horn. "I'm hungry."

Roxanne laughed. "Don't worry, Leo. They took a break and went and played for a bit before coming back for second breakfast."

"Keith says we're like hobbits," Ben said with a mouthful.

"Hobbits?"

Keith shrugged. "In the movie, they talk about second breakfast." He waved a hand. "It doesn't matter. Is everything okay? Lexi good?"

I tried not to smile too widely when I answered. "She's great. Just having a little nap, but she'll be out in a bit."

"Think Mom will dive off the diving board with me later?"

"I don't think so, buddy. Not this time."

"Why not?"

Everyone at the table stared at me. Lexi always went off the diving board, although only Ben would have known that. "She might." I shrugged, knowing full well I wouldn't let her do any such thing now that I knew she was pregnant. "We'll have to see how she feels when she wakes up."

I helped myself to some breakfast and while I ate, the kids finished their *second breakfast* and were back in the pool, Roxanne excused herself and it was just Keith and I left to talk business.

"About the investment." I might as well bring up the big issue right away. I stirred some more creamer into my coffee although I'd already had three cups and took a sip before I continued. "It's a lot of money."

"It is."

"It might take a bit to come up with it all." That was an understatement. "Were you able to come up with yours all at once? I realize that's a personal question. But I'm just trying to figure out—"

"It's okay. I actually had some savings and a few investments that I was able to cash in." Keith tipped his head, questioning me with his gaze. "What's up? Did you talk to Lexi yet?"

I nodded. Of course, we needed to talk about it some more, but preliminary talks were good. Once we got over the fight, that is.

"So, is she on board?" Keith picked at a piece of bacon one of the kids had left behind. "Because I know we agreed, but if it's a big problem, nothing is signed. We can find another investor. I have a few other—"

"No. She's good." I took a gulp of hot coffee. "I should say, she's good now. We still have a lot to discuss. But she agrees it's a great opportunity. It's just the investment dollars. I still have a few things to work out there."

Keith opened his mouth to say something else, but I didn't want to give him any excuse to even consider other investors. I quickly changed the subject to something that was more pressing anyway. "Did I see boats down by the water yesterday? Does Oasis have any or is that the neighboring resort?" I had an idea the other day and I was definitely going to need Keith's help to execute it. Especially if it was going to be as special as I hoped it would be.

~Lexi~

I LET the phone ring three times and was almost ready to hang up when Nicole answered on the fourth ring, out of breath and gasping for air.

"Nicole!" I clenched the phone to my ear a little tighter. "What's going on? Are you okay?" Was the baby coming early? Was she in labor? I needed to be there for the baby. *But if we stayed*...I couldn't think about it right now. "Are you having the baby?"

"No."

Relief washed through me. Followed quickly by renewed concern. "Then what's going on? You sound like—"

"We're just doing this thing the doula recommended to help with labor."

"This thing..." I knew the moment I asked. "Nicole! Please tell me you're not having sex."

"I can't tell you that."

"Why would you answer the...never mind." I shook my head and contemplated hanging up so they could finish whatever it was they were doing. But I needed to talk to her. "Can you take a...break...or something? There's something I want to talk about."

"Of course." I could always count on my best friend to put whatever she was doing on hold if I needed her. Even if it was sex. Fortunately, I didn't need her that often, but I knew she was always there if I did. I listened while she mumbled something to Ryan and heard the distinctive sound of kissing in the background before finally she came back on the line. "What's up? How's Vegas? Please tell me you're having fun."

"I am." It wasn't totally a lie. There'd been fun. "It's only been a few days, and—"

"You're not ready to come home, are you? I know how you feel about Vegas, but come on, Lex. Try to enjoy yourself for once. You need to have a little fun and if you can't have fun in Las Vegas, I'm not sure there's any hope for you at all. Remember, you had fun there once. And you met Leo and you—"

"Nic! I'm having fun. So much fun that I can't believe it. I'm out of control! Honestly, it's fine." Sometimes the only way to get her to listen was to yell. "I need to talk to you about something. But first, how's the baby? How do you feel?" I probably should have talked to her about my stuff first, because once you got Nicole talking about herself, all bets were off as far as getting a word in edgewise, but the second I got her on the phone, I'd needed a bit more time to tell her what I'd called to tell her. It was a chicken move, for sure. But I didn't care.

There was a long sigh and I could totally picture my friend with her hand on her back, stretching her exceedingly large belly forward in a dramatically stereotypical housewife fashion. "I'm enormous." She groaned. "I swear there's more than one baby in here. They keep telling me there's only one, but I was reading in a magazine the other day about a woman who went in to deliver one, and had three. *Three!* Can you even imagine? How do they miss *three?*"

"They don't," I said. "What magazine did you read that in?"

"I don't remember. But it's true. There were definitely three. There was a picture of her holding them all. I'd sue if that happened to me."

"So you think you're having triplets?" I rolled my eyes and was grateful she couldn't see me.

"No! Don't be ridiculous." Nicole paused. "But there's definitely two in there."

I had to swallow my laughter and it took me a minute to fully recover. "Right. Well, I'm glad you're feeling okay."

"Okay!?" She made a very unattractive half grunt, half choke noise. "If that's what you can call having a twelve-pound turkey pressing down on your bladder, kicking the crap out of your insides day in and day out. Seriously, Lex. You have *no* idea what this is like."

I couldn't help it, I laughed. Hard. When I recovered, I wiped the tears that had leaked from my eyes. "I have an almost twelve-year-old, remember? I have some idea what it's like." My hand cupped my growing belly that had seemed to have doubled since the last time I'd checked. "And I might have some—" I stopped myself from telling her about the baby. At least until we'd told Ben he was going to be a big brother. Besides, I needed to focus on the real reason for my call.

"You have some what?"

"Nothing." I shook my head; Nicole would never let it go. "I was just going to say that I have to make some plans for Ben's birthday in a few days." It was true, if not entirely the situation at hand. "And I have some news." Shifting gears was definitely the best approach. Although I wasn't sure how she was going to take it.

"You got married?" she shrieked through the line. "You bitch! You can't get married without me." She burst into messy loud sobs and I had to hold the phone away from my ear while she sniffed loudly into the receiver. I should have guessed how a hormonal and very pregnant Nicole, who was emotional on a good day, would react to such an ambiguous statement.

"Nic. Nic!" I raised my voice to be heard over her sobs. It was a damn good thing we hadn't gone through with the wedding. But she really wasn't going to like what I was going to tell her. "We didn't get married." I paused. She wasn't crying as hard, but she was still sobbing. "Did you hear me?"

A sniff, a snort, and she said, "Yes." She paused a beat and added, "How could you? I told you how important it was to me that my baby's godparents were married. And you're in Vegas. Lexi! If you're going to get married anywhere, it should be there."

My head spun. "Wait. What? Are you mad that I didn't get married? Because a second ago you were uncontrollably crying because you thought I had gotten married. Which is it?"

She grunted and there was silence before she finally said, "Both. Don't mess with me. I'm really pregnant and hormonal and I don't know what I want."

I chuckled a little. I, for one, couldn't wait until the baby was born and Nicole could go back to her normal level of neuroses. I couldn't imagine how Ryan was dealing with it. I was pretty sure a more patient man didn't exist.

I waited for Nicole to recover from her emotional rollercoaster and used the moment of quiet to walk with the cordless phone through the small garden area outside our room. It couldn't have been more different from the lush forest back home, but the cactus and desert flowers were gorgeous in a barren yet striking way of their own. There was so much potential still in the garden areas and despite my own indecision about moving to the desert, I knew I'd enjoy immersing myself in some of the challenges that Oasis would present. Leo was right: it was full of potential and maybe it was time for a change.

"So if you didn't call to tell me you got married, what's up?"

I took a breath and braced myself for another emotional outburst. There was no point dancing around it, not at this point. So I just said it outright. "Leo has been offered an amazing opportunity down here. We're considering it."

There was silence on the other end and for a moment I was concerned I might be responsible for Nicole going into early labor. I waited a beat. "Nic?"

"You're considering it?"

"Yes."

"An opportunity in Vegas?"

"Yes."

"Good."

"Good?" I was expecting any variety of responses, but *good* wasn't one of them.

"Yes," she said. "Good. Not that I want you to move, but let's face it."

"Face what?"

"You were never going to be able to stay at Lake Lillian forever, Lex. It was temporary."

"I don't understand. It wasn't temporary; it was..." I drifted off because on one hand her words confused me, but on the other hand, they made complete sense. She was right. Living in Lake Lillian long-term had never been the plan but after Uncle Ray died and I left Andrew, it just seemed like the place I needed to be. My sanctuary. And when Leo had come from Vegas to be with us, well...we'd just never left. But now... "I think you're right," I said after a moment.

"Of course I'm right. Besides, it's not like we've been in the same city for the last few years, and if you're living in one of my favorite places, it just gives me a good reason to come visit you so you can see your beautiful godbaby or babies."

I laughed again. "Of course you better come visit me. I need to have lots of baby cuddles and—" I almost told her again about the baby, but I bit my tongue just in time.

"But get married, would you?"

I shook my head before telling her about our near-miss nuptials. Before I hung up, I promised her that we'd at least think about it and by the time I tucked my cell phone back into my pocket and walked down the path that led to the main building, I felt a lot better about the choices Leo and I had to make, because whatever happened, I knew we'd make them together. As a family.

THE REST of the day passed quickly but I only saw Leo again in passing. He was busy with Keith: walking through the grounds, brainstorming ideas, and making lists. I decided a lazy afternoon was in order and allowed myself the luxury of lounging by the pool with Roxanne. I tried not to feel underdressed, or in this case, under made up when I was around her. She was a beautiful woman and every time I saw her, she was all dolled up, makeup on and hair done, perfectly in place. In sharp contrast to me, who considered mascara and lip gloss my *going out* face. Her clothes were carefully chosen while mine were whatever I had that would fit from the last time I went shopping, I don't know how long ago. But I wasn't judging based on outside appearances, because talking with Roxanne was actually a lot of fun. It was refreshing to hang out with someone who didn't know my history or my life back home. Besides, if we were going to stay, I'd be spending a lot of time with Roxanne.

"Don't take this the wrong way." I shifted the umbrella overhead. I was starting to feel the heat from the sun, and the last thing I wanted was a sunburn. "But what are you going to do at Oasis to keep yourself busy? Do you work?"

She laughed. "There's no way I could take that the wrong way. I'm actually talking to Keith about getting involved with some of the activities planning. There's a lot of opportunity for some fun family-oriented events and activities and I have a lot of good ideas about that, so he thought maybe we could turn it into a full-time position. I have experience in that area. Well, a little bit anyway. I used to manage a daycare."

I would have been less shocked if she'd told me she used to be a show girl. I sat up in my lounge chair and stared at her. "What? You?"

"I know. I don't really look like I worked with kids, but I did. Sort of." She tucked a stray hair back into the twist at the back of her head. "To be fair, I didn't really work with the children, but I worked around them. But ever since Evan and Ruby were born, I've had this strange maternal urge to do things and make memories. Does that make sense?"

I nodded, because it absolutely did. "Before Ben was born, I could never understand why some people liked to go pick out pumpkins in a field, or sing Christmas carols and all of that. But when he was born..." Everything changed. I didn't bother saying it; as mothers, we both knew it to be true. There were some things you couldn't put into words, and the way you felt about your children was generally one of those things.

"So what do you think you're going to do here?" Roxanne changed the subject. "Keith told me you're a teacher. I'm not sure what the requirements are for you to teach in Nevada, but maybe—"

"I think I'd be good taking a bit of time off," I answered,

surprising even myself. "At least until after the baby is born and then we'll have to see."

A smile split Roxanne's face. "So you decided to stay then? I mean, I know Keith said it was a done deal, but what he doesn't realize is that nothing is a done deal until the woman agrees."

I laughed and nodded. "It's a done deal. We still need to talk to Ben, but assuming he agrees with a little change and leaving his friends for a bit, I think we'll give it a shot. Change is good sometimes." We still needed to figure out the financing, and I still wasn't totally clear on what Leo's plan was for making that part of the equation add up, but I knew I didn't want him to sell the inn. I needed to talk to him a bit more, but the more I thought of it, the more I thought that we should use the inheritance from Uncle Ray to make up the difference.

"Well, I'm glad." Roxanne sat up abruptly and lunged for her cell phone that had started to chirp. I watched as her face underwent myriad expressions before finally settling into the warm smile I was getting used to. She set the phone down and jumped up. "Can I ask you for a favor?"

I nodded slowly. Something about the way she looked at me made me a bit nervous. "What's that?"

"I know this sounds ridiculous, but do you think you could try on one of my dresses for me?"

It did sound ridiculous. Especially considering we weren't really the same size. Roxanne definitely had a fuller bustline, and that was putting it mildly. Plus, with my thickening waist, it wasn't likely anything that she owned would fit me.

"I know what you're thinking." She grabbed my hand, yanking me up and out of my chair before I could object. "But I have the perfect dress for you."

I didn't even think to ask her why I would possibly need to try on one of her dresses until I stood in her gigantic walk-in closet, wearing the most gorgeous dress I'd worn in years: a halter top with an empire waist. Our difference in chest size didn't matter, although my breasts did seem noticeably larger than they had a few days ago. The fabric flowed over my belly, only skimming the curves that were becoming more apparent almost by the minute, it seemed.

"That color is gorgeous on you."

It really was. A deep fuchsia, it wasn't quite purple, but a deeper shade that shimmered brightly when I moved. I let Roxanne pile my hair on the back of my head in a simple yet surprisingly stunning up-do. She finished off my look with thin silver feathers that dangled from each lobe. I hardly recognized myself when she was finished. But in a totally good way.

"I don't know what to say," I breathed as I turned slowly in the mirror. "I look like me, only..."

"You're glowing."

I laughed. "I'm hardly glowing." I stopped turning and looked at her. "Thank you for this. But..." I shook my head, still confused as to what it was exactly we were doing.

"Don't worry about it." Roxanne grabbed my hand again and before I knew it, I was being pulled gently out of their suite and back down the path that led to the water.

"Where are we going?"

"There's something I want to show you."

I laughed, caught up in the complete silliness of what was happening. It had been so long since I'd spent time with a girlfriend just having fun, I'd almost forgotten how to do it. But when we turned the corner that led to the beach, my laughter died on my lips. I stopped so suddenly, Roxanne almost fell over.

What was going on?

CHAPTER TEN

~Leo~

I waited patiently while Roxanne led Lexi down the pathway. Even from where I sat on the gondola style boat, I could see how gorgeous she looked. I'd never seen her in a dress the color of the one she wore and with her increasingly curvy body, she looked like a goddess as she made her way, laughing, down to the water. I saw the exact moment she noticed Ben.

He was dressed somewhat formally in khaki shorts and a black polo shirt, his hair slicked back in my best effort to tame his locks that desperately needed a haircut. We were used to seeing him in jeans and old t-shirts or hoodies, so I'd hoped the effect would be dramatic and judging by the way Lexi stopped abruptly, I was right.

I couldn't hear what Ben said, but Lexi's hand flew to her mouth. I knew if I was closer, I would see the tears in her eyes, which meant Ben was carrying out his role according to plan. I swelled with pride at my boy. He made me a little prouder every day, if it was even possible. Ben reached out and extended his hand to his mother. She took it and he straightened his shoulders as he escorted her down to the dock.

Something resembling butterflies flipped in my stomach and it made me laugh. After all these years and everything we'd been through, I was nervous. It was crazy. But definitely a good sign.

The music I'd arranged with Keith started to play. That was my cue, so I hopped up, straightened my pants and made sure my shirt was tucked in just right, and my tie straight before I slipped my jacket on. Working in the mountains, it had been a long time since I'd worn a suit and tie, but I knew how Lexi liked it and if I was going to do things, I was going to do them right. I grabbed the lily I'd selected and made my way down the dock to meet the love of my life.

The moment she saw me, her eyes lit up and she tipped her head to the side in question. "Leo? What..." She turned to Ben, who watched his mother with absolute adoration. I knew what it meant to him to be included in the planning of what was about to happen. He'd been so excited, I was worried he'd let it slip to Lexi, so I'd kept him busy all day to make sure he didn't go anywhere near her. He was a good boy, but he was terrible at keeping secrets.

"Here she is, Dad." Ben extended his arm, Lexi's hand clasped in his, for me to take.

"Good job, son."

He beamed with pride and despite the confusion I could still see in Lexi's eyes, I also saw the emotion as she looked between us. I took her hand from Ben's and kissed the back of it before I handed her the lily.

"What's going on?" Lexi took a step toward me, but hesitated, looking back at Ben.

"You'll see." Ben rocked up on his toes and shoved his hands in his pockets. It was easy to see that he was busting to tell her some of the details. "Go with Dad."

I nodded and pulled gently on her hand to lead her back toward the boat. "Listen to your son." I squeezed her hand in assurance. "He's a smart boy."

We left Ben standing on the dock, but I knew the moment I helped Lexi aboard the gondola, he'd be moving into his next position.

"Here we are." I stopped in front of the gondola Keith had borrowed from the neighboring resort. It was one of the larger boats with an open bow that created a cozy sitting area, complete with cushions and a table that pulled out from the side. The crew area in the back housed the driver and the supplies we'd already stocked the boat with. I'd decorated the space with a few bouquets of lilies and they filled the air with their fragrance. Flameless candles flickered and a lantern sat, waiting to be lit when the sun went down.

"Leo, this is..."

I chuckled and helped her aboard and into the front sitting area. The sun was still out and it was warm, but soon enough it would be chilly and I was prepared for that, too. She sat on the cushions, and I pulled out a blanket. "For later," I said.

"Later? Are you going to tell me what's going on?"

"Patience, my darling."

I turned to the wheelhouse behind me and got the thumbs-up from Keith, our captain for the evening. I smiled when I saw Ben next to him. Just as I thought, it hadn't taken long for him to get in position. I nodded to Keith and turned back to my date.

The moment I sat down next to her, the engine fired up and we moved smoothly away from the dock. "I thought it might be kind of nice to see the resort from a different view." I smoothly put my arm around her. "Besides, with everything going on lately, we're long overdue for a little time alone, don't you think?"

~Lexi~

MY MIND SPUN and I couldn't keep up. From the moment Roxanne dragged me away from the pool to play dress up, to seeing my handsome son, and then...Leo.

I didn't know what to think. But when Leo sat down next to me and put his arms around my shoulders, it didn't matter what he was planning or doing. It just mattered that we were together and for that moment, everything was perfect.

The boat pulled away from the dock and moved out onto the lake. Soft music played from somewhere, and I snuggled into Leo. Besides our night out on the Strip, it had been way too long since we'd spent a romantic night together. And with a baby coming...I'd only just allowed myself to think of the baby in the future tense. Everything felt real now and if the way my stomach was suddenly growing and stretching was any indication, everything would be just fine with this baby.

"This is beautiful." I sat up just enough to look at the shoreline as we moved farther into the lake. The sun was just starting to set, which cast an orange glow over the water and the homes on the far end of the lake. "These houses are huge!"

"They are. I think that one's Celine Dion's. I guess the recession didn't affect things over there the way they did the hotels on this side of the lake."

I laughed. "I think when you're that rich, you're recession-proof. Look at that one." I pointed to an exceptionally large house. At first glance, I thought it must be another hotel, but it was definitely a house. I expected Leo to chime in, but when he didn't say anything, I turned to see him not looking in the direction I pointed, but staring directly at me. "Leo?"

He took my hand, pulling it down and into his lap. "I can't look at the houses."

I tilted my head in question.

"Because all I can look at is you," he continued. "There is nothing more beautiful, more magnificent, than you."

I blushed and looked away. "Leo, you're being—"

"Absolutely serious." He squeezed my hands until I faced him again. "I've never been more serious. The other night when I thought we were finally going to get married...I realized there were so many things wrong with what we were doing." I laughed because he was right. The laughter died on my lips when I realized he wasn't joining me. Instead, his face was a mask of seriousness. "I'm so glad you came down the aisle and called it off."

My heart sunk at his words and the realization of what he was saying.

"Lexi, I've never been happier that something didn't go the way I wanted it to." Nausea welled up inside me. I needed to get off the boat. "I'm glad I didn't marry you that night." I tried to yank my hand away, but he held fast.

My head shook of its own accord. "No," I whispered. "No. Why would you say—"

"Yes." Leo squeezed my hands. Tighter this time. "Look at me." I did so only because there was nowhere else to look when all I really wanted was to get off the boat and run away. *Why would he bring me on such a romantic boat ride just to break my heart in such a cruel way?*

Leo was still talking and it took me a moment to realize he was waiting for a response from me. "What?" I tried to focus on him, but his face was out of focus.

"Lex." His hand stroked my cheek. The touch of him was so

soft and sweet and totally at odds with the words that came from his mouth that a sob almost escaped me, but I caught it just in time. "There's one other thing that night in the chapel taught me. One really important thing."

"What's that?" I forced myself to sound casual when I felt anything but.

He smiled, that gorgeous, charming smile that first captivated my heart all those years ago. "When I saw you coming down the aisle to call everything off, I realized that there's nothing I want more than to see you walking down an aisle for real. Only the next time, you'll be walking toward me to become my wife, because I can't think of anything in this world I want more than to be married to you. We may have taken a twisted road to get to this point, but from the moment I met you, you've completely owned my heart, Lexi Titan. There is no one else in this world I want to be with."

He slipped away from me, but without letting go of my hands, got down on one knee right there in the bow of the boat. Tears welled up in my eyes. This time they were tears of joy and utter surprise, but I let them fall down my cheeks. Between my hormones and the wild ride of emotions over the last few days, I could barely keep up.

"Looking back on our life together," Leo continued, "I realize that our love deserves so much more than a hurried ceremony in some random chapel on the Strip." I laughed a little. "Our love deserves to be united as a family." Leo glanced up at something over my shoulder. I turned to follow his gaze and saw Ben behind me. His hands were shoved in his pockets as he watched us seriously. This time I couldn't help it; the emotions overwhelmed me and a sob escaped my mouth. Leo released one of my hands and I automatically reached for Ben, who came around to join us. Instead of sitting next to me, he remained standing and took Leo's free hand. Together, joined in a circle, I thought my heart would burst from joy. Leo winked at Ben, who grinned in a way that made him look just like a miniature version of his dad.

"So," Leo continued, "I don't know about you two, but I think it's long past time to make this official. Lexi...Ben...would you do me the honor of making me the happiest man in the world?"

Another sound somewhere between a sob and a laugh came out of my mouth and for a moment, I couldn't find any words.

"Well?"

We both turned to look at Ben, who looked confused and more than a little annoyed. "Are you going to say yes or what?"

I laughed again as tears streamed down my cheeks. "Yes. Of course, yes." Leo slipped the ring on my finger and stood as he pulled me up and into his arms. I clutched him to me, letting the tears soak his lapel. After a moment, we opened our arms and welcomed Ben into our circle. He squeezed between us, but only suffered the hug for a few moments before he pushed us apart.

He looked first at me and then his father before he shook his head.

"What?"

"The happiest man in the world?" Ben asked. "Really, Dad? You couldn't do better than that?"

I tried and failed to swallow my laughter, which quickly and inexplicably turned into uncontrollable sobs. I swiped at my tears, but it was pointless.

"Mom?"

"I'm fine."

When I couldn't stop crying, Leo put his arm around my shoulders and guided me back to settle into the cushions. A tissue appeared from somewhere and Leo sent Ben to get me a bottle of water. It took a few minutes, but finally I pulled myself together. After one final dab at my eyes, I looked at their concerned faces. Ben looked so much like his dad, it took me off guard sometimes, and I had the brief question of what the new baby might look like. "I'm fine," I said to my boys. "Honestly. I'm more than fine. I can't believe you guys planned all of this. It was so sweet, but I have to tell you, it's not nice to do something so emotional to a pregnant woman. My hormones are totally out of con—"

I realized too late that I'd slipped. I stopped talking and looked to Leo, who only lifted his eyebrows and turned to Ben, whose mouth was open.

"What do you mean...pregnant?"

Leo grabbed my hand and grinned so broadly I thought his face would split. "You're going to be a big brother," he said.

Ben didn't react right away. Not that I could blame him. We'd told him once before that he was going to be a brother, and that hadn't worked out the way we'd planned. We'd kept the other pregnancies a secret, but he was a smart boy. I'm sure he must have known on some level.

"You mean..." He looked between us. "You're going to have a baby?"

I nodded, still watching his reaction carefully. "We're just past three months, so this time..." I couldn't finish what I was thinking, but I didn't need to.

"I'm going to be a brother?" We nodded. "And you're going to *finally* get married?" We nodded again and Ben jumped up to do a fist pump. "Best. Day. Ever. And it's not even my birthday yet!"

As I looked at the two loves of my life with a new baby safe in my belly, I couldn't agree more.

~Leo~

EVERYTHING HAD GONE OFF PERFECTLY. Ben had been amazing. Lexi had reacted just as I'd planned. Well, almost as planned. There was no planning for the hormonal reaction of a pregnant woman. But that didn't matter; it only added to the night. After we told Ben about the baby, I brought out the sparkling apple juice and the three of us cuddled under a blanket as Keith drove the boat slowly around the lake.

The water turned orange, and then pink as we watched the sunset. Finally the stars came out and I lit the lantern for a bit more light as we took in the sights of the resorts and mansions on the shoreline.

It was a beautiful night and with my arms around my son and my soon-to-be wife who was pregnant with my child, I couldn't imagine anything more perfect than that moment.

Lexi and I could have driven around all night, but when Ben finally fell asleep on my lap, I turned and gestured to Keith that it was time to head back to the dock. He'd been fantastic about donating his captain skills, but he was probably eager to get back to shore, too. Besides, I was more than ready to get my fiancée alone.

Just thinking the word in my head, it still seemed surreal, which was crazy because we'd been in love and living together for years. But somehow now that it was going to be official, it seemed different. And so much better.

"Let me take him," I said when the boat was finally docked. I scooped Ben up in my arms and with a nod of thanks to Keith, Lexi and I headed back up to our suite. "I'll put him to bed and be right back."

Lexi smiled and I walked through the spacious room to the door that was Ben's bedroom. Fortunately it was a large suite, almost as big as our entire cabin home back in Canada. There was one more empty room on this side of the suite with the master located on the opposite side of the living room. It would be big enough for our expanding family. At least for a while. After the resort got going, I'd find us a real home nearby in the village where we could really put down some roots. It wouldn't be the same as the cabin, but it would be wonderful and we could always visit the lake and the mountains. Especially if I could find some way to hang onto the inn and hire Seth full-time to run it in my absence. That little place had a piece of my heart already, and I wasn't ready to give it up. Not if I didn't have to.

I just didn't know how I could make that happen.

I tucked Ben under his covers and slipped out of his room without waking him. It had been a big night and he was a good sleeper; I knew I didn't have to worry about him waking up. Which was a good thing, because when I walked into the living room and saw Lexi, her back to me as she sat on the couch and gazed out the window, my body reacted hard and fast to the sight of her. Particularly her long, slim neck, the creamy white skin left exposed by the artful pile of hair on the back of her head. I made a quick mental note to thank Roxanne for her handiwork. My fiancée looked even more gorgeous than normal, and I never would have thought that possible.

I didn't think I'd made any noise as I made my way across the carpet, but she turned, sensing my presence as I came up behind the couch. The smile on her face, the total look of joy, only fueled my desire. Before she could say anything, I bent and kissed her neck. Softly at first, I let my lips move across her bare skin, licking and tasting until I heard the telltale moan that meant her eyes were closed and she was surrendering to me and my attentions. Encouraged, I slipped one hand to her other shoulder, and around to her chin, pulling her head down to expose more of her neck.

My kisses grew more urgent, and my tongue traveled her sweet skin, up behind her ear, tracing it, before dipping briefly inside. She shivered, hard. I knew exactly how I was affecting her. I suckled her lobe into my mouth and my free hand moved around her to cup her breast in my palm. Her body was changing, her breasts definitely growing more luscious every day. I noticed a difference even from the previous day when we'd been together. Was it possible for a body to change so quickly?

Fortunately, the fabric of the dress was loose enough for me to slide my hand easily inside. She moaned again when my thumb stroked over her nipple, pebbling it into a hard peak. Once again, I focused on the skin of her neck while my hand squeezed and kneaded her breast. She turned her head, desperate to meet my lips with her own. I complied and took her mouth in a hot, hungry kiss. She turned on the couch until she was on her knees facing me.

My hands slipped through her hair, holding her head firmly to me; a need to claim her as mine ran fiercely through my blood. "I love you so goddamned much."

My voice was thick and the words came out gravelly and raspy but she smiled the sweetest smile and spoke with just as much heat. "I can't imagine wanting or needing a man as much as I do you."

That's all it took. I was around the couch in a heartbeat. I swept my woman up in my arms and took her to our bedroom, where we consummated everything we'd just promised each other.

CHAPTER ELEVEN

~Lexi~

I couldn't wait. No. I *wouldn't* wait.

After the most romantic proposal I could have ever dreamed up and then telling Ben about the baby, I was done waiting. I was ready to get married!

Waking up an engaged woman, I was pretty sure I could take on the world. As soon as the sun started to creep through the cracks of the curtains, I was ready to start planning the start of our new life. Of course, no one else was ready to plan with me as they were all still sleeping, so I spent a half hour walking through the gardens, or what would be the gardens when they were finished. There was so much potential, and not that I knew anything at all about gardening in the desert, but I couldn't help but get excited about learning. I was ready for a change, too. As much as I loved teaching, it was always good to try new things.

I stopped at the top of the hill and looked down at the pools and lake below. The wind started to pick up and I wrapped my sweater tighter around my body, noting how it wouldn't be long before it wouldn't tie up at all. If the early signs were any indication, this baby was definitely going to be a big one.

I scanned the lake, and the dark clouds that were rolling in from the far side of the lake. That type of weather was pretty normal for the mountains, especially in November. In fact, those dark clouds would mean snow for us back in Canada. But in Nevada, I wasn't used to seeing such clouds. There was probably going to be a storm of some sort. Roxanne had mentioned that occasionally there'd be some pretty wild windstorms, but those clouds looked like rain.

There were a few kayaks along the shoreline of the neighboring resort, and they must have spotted the storm as well because as I watched, they turned around and paddled back, ending their sunrise trip. Farther across the lake, toward the far end where there weren't any resorts or many houses, I could see the shape of what was probably a boat. But no doubt, they'd seen the clouds, too.

My eyes traveled up the small beach and up to the decks and patios that would soon hold families on holidays or couples on a romantic getaway. I'd seen the potential in Oasis from the beginning. I may not have agreed with it right away, but I knew in my heart, it was the right move for our family. It was time to start fresh and with a baby on the way, there couldn't be a more perfect time. Oasis was going to be spectacular and it was definitely different than the Lake Lillian Inn. Not better...but different. The inn was special, too. And that's why I knew Leo couldn't sell it. It was the one thing that stopped me.

I couldn't let Leo sell the inn. Even if we weren't going to be living in Canada, he had to keep it. I knew Leo would never ask me for any of Uncle Ray's inheritance, but I also knew exactly what Uncle Ray would want me to do with it.

I had a few calls to make but just knowing everything was going to work out made me smile.

It would be perfect.

Everything was going to be just perfect.

IT WAS torture waiting for Leo to wake up, but he finally did and I was ready for him. He walked out of the bedroom, droplets of water still clinging to his hair from his shower, and it was all I could do to keep my hands off him, he looked so sexy. My pregnancy hormones must have kicked into high gear. Or maybe it was just my state of mind. Either way, there'd be time for that later and I forced myself to tamper my desire.

"Good morning." He wrapped his arms around me and kissed me on the lips. "Both you and Ben slept in today. I know it was a late night, but still."

"Ben's still sleeping?" I nodded as I handed him a cup of coffee. "That's unusual. He's always up at the crack of dawn, which is unusual in its own way for a boy his age."

I laughed because it was a running joke with us that Ben was the only morning person out of all of us and we kept waiting for him to outgrow it and start sleeping in, but he never did.

But I wasn't worried. It was good for Ben to get a little more sleep. "Did you sleep well?" I asked Leo.

"I did until I rolled over and saw you weren't there. Did you have trouble sleeping?"

I smiled and shook my head. "Not at all. I was just too excited to stay in bed this morning. I've been very busy already." I slid the piece of paper with the figures on it that had been emailed to me earlier from the lawyer who'd handled Uncle Ray's estate. "I know it's not much," I said. "And I know it won't be enough. But with our savings, it should be enough for our share of Oasis."

He looked at me, confusion on his face. "No." He shook his head and slid the paper back toward me. "We don't need it, Lex. I had the money figured out."

I could tell by the look on his face that he, in fact, did not have it figured out. Or at least not as completely as he would have liked.

"This will make it happen without selling the inn," I said. "You can't sell it."

He shook his head and smiled sadly. "Lexi..."

"No. I won't let you. Even if we're here. Seth can run it. You've set it up so well, you don't need to be there every day anymore anyway. Besides, we'll still have the cabin and we'll be able to go back in the summer to spend time at the lake. You can check on it then and make sure everything is running well." He opened his mouth to say something, but I cut him off. "Leo, the inn is too important to sell. It represents..." Tears sprang to my eyes. "Well...it represents *us*."

His smile was so sweet that I knew he felt the same way. "But financially...I'm not sure if it makes sense."

"Of course it does." I tapped my fingers on the paper and tried to feel more confident then I felt. Financially it was going to be a stretch, no matter what we did. "Leo, I've been sitting on that money for a while now because I wasn't sure what to do with it. But now I know."

"It's your money."

"It's *our* money." I clasped his hands over the eating bar and looked into his eyes. "And I can't imagine doing anything else with it. We need to do this for our family."

~Leo~

SHE WAS AN AMAZING WOMAN. There was no denying that. I counted my blessings every day that she'd chosen me to fall in love with and that fate had pulled us together again after driving us apart. Our story was one of many twists and turns, but everything was finally coming together just the way it should be.

I left Lexi in the suite to wake Ben up and headed off in search of Keith. It was time to make everything official and start some real work on the Oasis. Especially if we were going to get up and running in time for Christmas.

Outside, the wind whipped the palm trees with a ferocity that was troubling. I'd spent a lot of time in Nevada, and I knew enough to know that a desert storm with wind like this usually brought a lot of trouble with it. Talking to Keith would have to wait. First, the grounds would need to be secured.

Glad I'd grabbed a sweater before leaving the suite, I tugged it over my head and headed for the pool area. Fortunately there weren't any guests to worry about and most of the lounge chairs around the pool were still stacked next to the snack shacks where they'd been delivered. I gathered up the few cushions that had blown off and tucked them into a storage shed before I headed up the stairs and into the main building.

"It's crazy out there," Keith greeted me the moment I walked in. "I've been out front, pulling in whatever isn't tied down. We can't afford to lose anything right now."

"I just grabbed the pool cushions," I said. We walked together down the hall toward the offices, talking about what other areas of concern we had for the storm, and laughing at our good luck that the resort didn't have guests to worry about so we could use it as a dry run for future storms or emergencies.

"Keith!" We stopped and turned to see Roxanne running

across the marble lobby toward us. She wore only a bathrobe, her hair flying behind her. "They're gone!"

"Who's gone?"

Keith caught her and held her arms but I could see the way Roxanne shook. She looked to me, searching for what, I didn't know. Her eyes were wild and unfocused.

"The kids. I went to wake them up and their beds were empty. I can't find them anywhere."

Instantly, the hair on the back of my neck stood up and an icy lump formed in my throat, but I waited.

"They're probably in the kitchen or the restaurant getting—"

"No." Roxanne's hair flew in her face with the force of her head shaking. "They're not there. I've looked everywhere."

Ben.

I reached for my cell phone to call Lexi. There was no doubt that Ben was fast asleep in his bed, enjoying a very rare sleep in, but I needed to be sure. But before I could dial, Lexi's beautiful face appeared on my screen. An incoming call. The lump in my throat grew and I coughed loudly to clear it before I answered. I knew without a doubt exactly what I was going to hear. "Lexi?"

"Ben's gone."

~Lexi~

HE WAS GONE.

Gone.

Where could he be?

Irrationally, I pulled all the coverings off his bed as if he'd somehow be hiding between the sheet and the comforter. I flung open the closet for at least the fifth time.

Where *was* he?

When I'd called Leo, he told me not to go anywhere, that he was coming back. I paced the room, looking for something—anything—that would tell me where my son had gone. I knew it was unusual that he was sleeping in. Ben never slept in. But it was also unusual for him to disappear.

And by unusual, it was flat out unheard of.

"Lexi?"

I ran into the living room and into Leo's arms. "Where is he?" I mumbled into his chest. "What's going on?"

He untangled himself from me and led me to the couch. "We'll find him. Evan and Ruby are missing too. They likely went off together and are hiding out during the storm. I'm sure it's fine. They're probably in one of the outbuildings. Keith and I are going to go look for them before the storm gets worse."

"I'm coming."

"Lexi, I don't—"

I narrowed my eyes to silence him. He knew enough to know he couldn't keep me from being part of the search party and he was smart enough not to even try.

"Grab a sweater," he said. "It's cold out there. The storm really picked up."

The storm.

"Do you think they're okay?" I asked, mostly to keep myself from obsessing as we left the suite and headed toward the pools and the outbuildings there. "I mean, it's early. Where would they have gone? You did put Ben to bed last night—he was sleeping. You don't think someone—"

"Lexi." Leo turned around and grabbed me by the upper arms. "Stop. They're fine. They're going to be just fine. Panicking or creating worst-case scenarios isn't going to help. We need to stay calm and think like the kids."

I nodded. Of course he was right. We needed to stay calm. I

scanned the grounds from where we stood. The wind whipped my hair around my face. The pools were up the stairs, the basketball and tennis courts to the right. The main building was to the left. The beach was behind us. I turned back to the stairs that led to the pools. The kids had spent the vast majority of their time there since we'd arrived. It seemed like the logical place to look. We hustled up the stairs and toward the outbuildings.

"I'll check the boys' room," Leo said. "You check the girls'. Maybe they took cover from the storm."

I nodded, although it didn't make sense or add up. But then again, at the moment, nothing made sense. The girls' change room was empty. I also popped into the vacant snack bar building and Leo checked the storage shed. All empty. When we came out and regrouped, Keith and Roxanne were there.

"Nothing?"

Leo shook his head. "The pool area is all clear."

"So are the courts." Keith had to yell to be heard over the howling wind. "Joanne is checking all the rooms just in case they decided to play hide-and-seek or something like that."

"I just don't understand," Roxanne cried. "Where could they have gone? Why would they sneak off?"

"We have to think like them," I said, although I couldn't even begin to imagine how. "What reason would they have for sneaking out? Is there something they would want to do that we wouldn't let them?"

Roxanne shook her head. "They know they have the run of the place. What would we have said no to?"

"The boat." All heads turned to Keith. The look on his face said it all. "Evan wanted to go last night when we went out on the boat."

The boat? Something pricked at me, but I couldn't think. Keith was still talking.

"I told him he couldn't come," Keith explained. "It was a special night."

Leo nodded and added, "But how could they? They're kids. They wouldn't have the first clue how to operate a boat."

"That's the thing." Keith scratched his head. "Ben was asking all kinds of questions last night. You know, before the big moment."

The boat.

There was a boat on the lake that morning. At dawn. It was headed away from the resort, to the secluded part of the lake. Toward the storm. "Ben!" I took off running toward the water, hoping upon hope that I'd see the boat still tethered on the dock where we'd left it last night, but knowing in my heart that I wouldn't.

~Leo~

"Lexi!"

I hollered after her, but she wasn't slowing down. There was no way Ben would be on the boat. But the way Lexi was running to the dock, she obviously didn't feel the same way.

"Lexi," I called again. "Slow down. He's not on the—"

The boat was gone.

I swung around to yell at Keith. He must not have tied it up securely. The wind and waves must have jarred it lose.

"I know what you're thinking." Keith's face turned a sickly shade of white. "But I tied it up tight. There's no way..."

"Are they...oh my God!" Roxanne joined us on the empty dock. She looked wildly between us all. "Do something! Keith! Where's the boat?"

Keith looked helplessly up and down the dock and scanned

the water, putting his hand up to shield his eyes against the wind. "It's...I know I...dammit."

"It's out there."

She spoke so softly, I almost didn't hear her over the wind and storm. Lexi pointed into the water in the opposite direction of the resorts and houses. The far end of the lake. I moved closer to her and stood behind her. "What do you mean, Lex? Did you see it?"

She nodded and something inside me cracked. "This morning, while I was waiting for you to wake up, I noticed a boat headed that way. I thought it was strange, but now..."

"It's the kids."

She turned; tears streamed down her face. "It's the kids," she repeated.

I wanted nothing more than to pull her into my arms, but there was no time. The kids needed me more. I squeezed her arm in a way I hoped felt more reassuring to her than it did to me and turned to Keith. "Who monitors the lake? Who do we call? We have to get those kids out of there."

Keith was already punching numbers into his phone. "The lake is privately owned. There are warnings posted all the time to keep something like this from happening. I don't watch it very carefully yet because we don't have the—yes, hello." He shifted his attention to the phone and told whoever was on the other end of the line what was happening. I listened with half an ear and turned to Lexi at the same time, pulling her tight against my chest. She shivered violently. Whether from the wind or fear, I couldn't be sure.

"We have to get you inside," I said. "You're freezing."

"I'm not going anywhere."

I'd expected as much. I wrapped my arms tighter, trying to infuse my warmth into her.

"Okay, they're sending out a rescue boat." Keith appeared

next to me, his arm around Roxanne. "They'll be okay." The four of us nodded in turn, not taking our eyes off the churning water in front of us. The early day sky was so dark with storm clouds, we couldn't see to the other side of the lake. The rain started just as we saw the bright light of a rescue boat move across the water, cutting through the waves, headed to the far end of the lake, and hopefully the children. Nobody moved, despite the sting of the rain. "They'll be okay," Keith said again.

I held Lexi closer. They had to be okay. They had to be.

~Lexi~

I WATCHED the light move across the water until the storm swallowed it from my view. They needed to hurry. The boat needed to move faster. My baby was out there. Ben.

I felt as if I couldn't breathe, but somehow oxygen kept filling my lungs. If Leo hadn't been holding me up, I wouldn't have been able to stand on my own. The stifling weight of helplessness covered me, weighing me down so I was frozen in place as I stared at the water. I barely felt the sting of the driving rain, and refused to look away from where I'd last seen the light of the rescue boat.

It was taking too long. They should have them by now. Something was wrong.

I squeezed my eyes shut. Just for a moment. Just long enough to force the negative thoughts from my mind.

"There!"

My eyes snapped open, just as Leo repeated himself. "There. I see the light."

The boat was on its way back. Headed directly toward us.

But did they have the kids? I dared not speak. Instead, I chanted a simple mantra in my head over and over again.

Be okay. Be okay. Be okay.

It took forever for the boat to make its way through the rough water. Finally, it was there. A crew member yelled and threw a rope to Keith, who caught it and hauled the boat closer to the dock. Leo unwrapped his arms from me to help bring in and tie up the boat.

"It's nuts out there," the crew man said. "Your dock was the closest one. We'll ride it out until—"

"The kids?" Leo interrupted him. "Did you find them?"

Just then, another crew member, a female, appeared from inside the boat, with three smaller figures, all wrapped in blankets.

The kids! They were okay.

"We got them," she said. "Lucky, too. The boat washed up on the far shore with the wind." She helped the kids to the dock. First Evan and Ruby, who ran into Roxanne's waiting arms, and then Ben. He was there in my arms, pressed against my chest. He was cold and wet and...whole. Wrapped tightly in my embrace, I didn't plan on ever letting him go.

I vaguely heard the rescuer, still talking. Saying something about high winds, danger, capsizing. It didn't matter. I had my baby. I had Ben in my arms and I was never letting him go.

"Ben, thank God." Leo was there; his arms surrounded us in a cocoon that I happily could have stayed in forever. "Let's get inside. This is insane."

And then Ben was pulled from my arms, but only to be lifted into those of his father. Leo grabbed my hand and together we half walked, half jogged through the storm up to the main building.

. . .

ONCE I WAS in the warmth, and we were all wrapped in blankets on the couches in the lounge with cups of hot tea and hot chocolate in front of us, Leo and Keith sent Joanne to our individual suites to fetch dry clothing for everyone. It was unspoken that we weren't going anywhere. Roxanne couldn't stop kissing her kids' heads, which had started to earn her dirty looks from each of them in turn. Ben suffered my attentions in silence, but I was pretty sure it was because he was as shaken up as I was about the whole experience.

"I can't believe I almost lost you," Roxanne said to Evan. Not that I was counting, but it must have been at least the twentieth time she'd said that.

"Mom." Evan tried to pull away from her. "We're fine. You didn't lose—"

"Stop sassing your mom." Keith gave the boy a stern look. "What you three did was inexcusable. Putting your mothers through that type of worry...putting all of us through that," he amended. It was easy to see how much Keith cared for Roxanne's kids. "The least you can do is sit there and put up with the attention."

"The very least," Leo added. "And then we're going to talk about what happened."

Ben ducked his head into my chest and snuggled deeper. I knew I wasn't going to like what Ben had to tell me about what happened because I knew the way only a mother does that he was not only involved but very likely the ringleader.

We drank our warm drinks and ate the muffins that had been laid out for us and when everyone's bellies were full and the feeling had returned to our cold toes, it was finally time to talk.

"Evan, let's start with you," Keith said. "Do you want to tell us what happened?"

"Why me?"

"You're the oldest." Keith looked at him pointedly. "And I know you wanted to go for a boat ride. What were you thinking? You can't take a boat out on your own. You're only thirteen years old. You could have been—"

"It was me."

All eyes turned toward me or more specifically, the little boy sitting with me.

"What are you saying, Ben?" Leo, who hadn't been very far away, moved even closer and took Ben's hand. "You have to tell us the truth, okay?"

"I know." Ben nodded solemnly. "I am telling the truth. It wasn't Evan. It was me. I knew he wanted to go for a ride and I thought it would be cool if I took him. So we got up really early and went out. We were supposed to be back before you woke up so you wouldn't find out."

"How did you know how to drive it?" Roxanne asked the question, but I already knew the answer. Ben was a smart kid. He paid attention.

"Last night I watched what Keith did."

"And you asked a lot of questions." Keith nodded knowingly and then shook his head in bewilderment. "Damn."

"Damn is right." Leo's mouth was pressed into a thin line. "Ben, this is not okay. You could have been killed. You put everyone at risk. Do you realize how serious this is?"

Ben nodded and I could see his lip tremble as he tried not to cry. "I'm sorry." He craned his head around so he looked at me. I nodded in support and he whipped around to look at everyone else in turn. "I really am," he said. "I didn't mean for anything bad to happen and...and..." He dissolved into a puddle of tears and I pulled him tight to me again. For all his bravado, he was still my little boy.

"I think we all understand how sorry you are, kiddo." I

pressed a kiss to the top of his head. Everyone murmured in understanding.

"I think we do," Roxanne said. "I'm just glad everyone's okay. Why don't you kids go back to our suite and watch a movie?" The kids, smart enough to know when they were being let off the hook, didn't have to be asked twice. Ben gave me another quick hug and the three of them took off, leaving us alone to decompress.

"I don't think I've ever been so scared," Roxanne said when they were out of earshot. "Thinking that something might have..." She shook her head. "I just can't think about it."

"I agree," I said. "It makes you realize how short life is." I reached for Leo's hand and wrapped my fingers through his. "And it makes you think that maybe you shouldn't wait for a perfect moment that might never come in order to be happy."

"What are you saying?" Leo watched me intently, his dark eyes full of question.

A smile crept across my face as I told him what I'd been thinking ever since I had Ben back in my arms. "I'm saying that I don't want to wait another day. It's long past time that I became your wife. Let's get married. Today."

CHAPTER TWELVE

~Leo~

There was no way I could say no to a request like that. I felt as if I'd already been waiting far too long to have Lexi as my wife and after the fear of the morning and thinking we may have lost Ben, nothing could keep me from waiting any longer to make it official.

After Lexi made her announcement, Roxanne declared that she had "the perfect dress" and Keith said he would find a minister or justice of the peace or anyone else who could perform the ceremony, which we didn't think would be too much of a problem given our location. Everyone hopped into action, happy to have something positive to do to distract them from the stress of the morning. Pretty soon people were yelling, making lists and arranging a car to take Lexi and I to get the marriage license we'd overlooked in our quickie attempt at a ceremony the other night. Lexi was at the center of it all, laughing, smiling, and looking every bit the radiant bride.

I stood and watched her for a few moments, in awe at the resilience and flexibility of the amazing woman in front of me. She'd always been the perfect blend of strength and softness. Without putting too fine a point on it, she was incredible. Everything I'd ever wanted. And in a few hours, she'd finally be legally mine. I crossed the room to her and extended my hand to her. "Can I borrow you for a second?"

She smiled up at me, her nose crinkling just a little. "Of course." She allowed me to take her out to the lobby area where the very small staff we had was hard at work setting up for the ceremony. "Is everything okay?" she asked when we were alone by the picture window, looking out to the storm that had started to fade out.

"Everything's fine." I kissed her on the nose. "I just wanted to check in with you."

She laughed. It had been awhile since I'd seen her so carefree and happy. Which was why it was going to be hard to ask the question I wasn't sure I wanted the answer to. But I knew it was the right thing to do. "I just wanted to make sure that you're sure about all of this."

"Of course I am." She laughed. "Why wouldn't I be?" The smile melted off her face. "Are you sure? You're not having second thoughts, are you?"

"Of course not," I said quickly. "Lexi, I've been committed to you for years—that's not going to change. With or without a ceremony." I squeezed her hand in mine. "What I meant was, are you sure you want to get married without your friends here? Without Nicole or Enid?"

It was a question that had pricked at me from the moment she'd announced her desire to get married right away. After Uncle Ray passed, Lexi had been left without family: Her parents had died when she was just a girl. Her first husband, Andrew, had disappeared from their lives when the truth came out that Ben was my son and not his the way everyone had pretended. As far as Lexi's family went, Ben and I were it. Except for her best friends. They should be next to her on her wedding day.

Her eyes welled up with tears and she swiped at them before she shook her head. "Nicole can't travel right now. She's going to have a baby any day. Besides, she'll just be so happy to hear that we're finally doing it and will make suitable godparents after all." She smiled. "And Enid wouldn't be able to leave the store on such short notice." She shook her head again. "No. They'll understand. Besides, remember what we did for Nicole's wedding, with the camera and the computer?"

I nodded. I remembered. We'd hooked up a Skype-type of chat so Nicole's mom could watch her get married despite the fact that she was back in Canada and the wedding was in Vegas. "We could absolutely do that," I said. "As long as you're okay with it."

"I'm more than okay with it." Her grin told me everything I needed to know. "I just want to marry you and finally be your wife. And I really don't want to wait even one more day before that happens."

"I'll make it happen."

"Good." She gave me a quick kiss and pushed me away playfully. "Now get out of here. You're not supposed to see the bride before the wedding. It's bad luck."

"Okay, okay." I reluctantly let go of her, but before I left, I said, "But, there is nothing that will ruin this day. Nothing."

~Lexi~

THE AFTERNOON HAD BEEN a whirlwind of making plans and finalizing last-minute arrangements, but everything had fallen into place. Even the weather had decided to cooperate. It was still cool but the sun was out and the wind had died down, bringing a beautiful evening and a sky full of stars.

For the second day in a row, I found myself in Roxanne's room while she curled and pinned up my hair into a beautiful twist before she turned her attentions to my makeup. "Light on the eye shadow, okay?" I had experience with friends trying to alter my appearance in the past. Particularly with Nicole dressing me up in tight, short dresses and trying to turn me into something I wasn't.

"Don't worry about a thing," Roxanne cooed and grabbed another brush. "I'm only going to accent your gorgeousness. You will be the most beautiful bride anyone has ever seen."

I believed her, but it didn't mean I wasn't a little bit nervous. Although, I couldn't figure out why I'd be nervous to marry Leo.

Finally.

I know I'd said it was fine not to have Nicole there for the ceremony, but I couldn't help feel a twinge of regret that she wasn't there to hold my hand and support me. Not that I had anything to need support for. Not really. But still, there was something about your wedding day that made you yearn for your best friend.

Abba's "Dancing Queen" filled the room and I immediately broke into a smile. "Can you pass me my phone? That's Nicole."

Roxanne laughed but handed me my cell. "Your best friend has Abba as a ringtone?"

"If you knew Nicole, it would make total sense." I answered the call. "Nic! I'm so glad you called." I'd already spoken with her once to let her know about the wedding and make the arrangements for the video call so she could watch the ceremony, but despite that, it was good to hear her voice.

"Of course I called," she said through the line. "It's your wedding day. And if I can't be there in person, I'm damn well going to be with you over the phone as much as I can. Now what's going on? Is your hair done yet? What about makeup?"

I blinked hard to hold back the tears that suddenly sprang up. "My hair's done," I managed.

"Don't you cry," Roxanne warned, pointing an eye shadow brush at me. "I'm almost done with your eyes."

"Are you crying?"

I shook my head in answer to Nicole's question and then quickly said, "No. Well, not really. I'm just so emotional."

"Of course you are," Roxanne said. "Your hormones are going crazy."

"Hormones? What hormones?" Nicole's voice went up an octave. "I have hormones! But that's because I'm pregnant. Pregnant women have—wait."

I waited.

When Nicole spoke again, her voice was eerily calm. "Why do you have hormones, Lexi?"

I smiled and winked at Roxanne before I answered her. "I was going to wait until after your baby was born," I said. "But I'm pregnant."

There was silence on the other end and I knew exactly what Nicole was thinking. She was thinking of the other pregnancies and how they ended in sadness.

"It's okay, Nic. The doctor said I should be past the danger zone with this one. And I feel great but my belly is growing at an incredible rate, so that has to be a good sign, right?"

She was silent for another moment. "You're sure? I mean, you know I'm excited for you, but..."

"You're worried," I finished for her. "I know. I was, too. But this time is different. We haven't had an ultrasound yet, but I just know everything is okay. Nicole, I just know it."

I waited and finally got the response I was looking for. Nicole whooped and hollered into the phone; her voice rang loud and clear across the line. "Lexi, that's fantastic! I'm so excited for you. Our babies will be the same age. They can grow up together and—well, even if you're in Vegas and we're here. More reasons to have lots of visits, right?"

"Right." The stupid hormonal tears sprang into my eyes again. I did my best to dab at them before Roxanne could see, but it was no use; she noticed and was on top of me with a cotton ball and a fresh swipe of makeup.

"Why don't we put her on FaceTime so I can get back to work?"

"Yes," Nicole agreed. "Do that. I want to pretend I'm there. Besides, I have to make sure you're putting enough eye shadow on. You know that Lexi's eyes pop when you use a green shadow?"

I shook my head in horror at Roxanne, but she only laughed and took the phone from my hand to prop it up on the table. When Nicole's face appeared on the screen, I smiled and blew her a kiss. For better or for worse, my best friend was there. Everything was going to be perfect.

~Leo~

I HAD to hand it to Keith. He'd really pulled things together. The lobby of the Oasis had been totally transformed. Flowers were on every available surface and candles flickered all around me, lighting up the space with a romantic, intimate glow. Beautiful music floated through the room from some hidden speakers and instead of chairs, our very few guests and witnesses stood in a semi-circle around the altar area where I waited with the justice of the peace for my bride.

The day had been a whirlwind but I'd never felt so calm and at peace than that moment. When the music changed and everyone turned to look, my heart leapt a little, but only because I couldn't wait to actually make Lexi my wife. The small crowd parted, revealing the most amazing sight I'd ever seen. Ben, dressed handsomely in black dress pants and a blue dress shirt, stood tall and proud with the most beautiful woman I'd ever seen on his arm. His mother.

I always thought Lexi was gorgeous, but dressed in a pale cream floor-length dress made of some sort of flowy fabric that hugged her breasts and floated over the rest of her luscious body, she was beyond stunning. Her hair was once again piled on top of her head, with strands trailing to her bare shoulders.

My breath was in my throat as she approached me. "Hey," she whispered.

"Hey yourself."

I looked down to Ben, who stood between us, his back straight, his hand trembling as he reached out to give me his mother's hand. "Thank you, buddy. You did a great job."

"Keith said it's my job to give her away." Ben's lower lip trembled, but he swallowed hard. "But I can't give her away because she's already ours. So I'm bringing her to you so we can all be an official family."

I shook my head in wonderment. When had he grown up so much? "Absolutely, Ben. We've always been a family, but it's way past time to make this official." I bent down and whispered in his ear. "I'm so proud of you."

Ben nodded and I took Lexi's hand from his before he took a half step back.

We'd both agreed on a short ceremony. Neither of us

wanted or needed anything fancy and although we'd wanted to include Ben in the vows, he'd begged off the way an pre-teen boy was apt to do. A wish we both respected.

I didn't hear most of what the justice of the peace said; I was too busy staring at my bride. When he paused in his speech and Lexi turned to look at me with a question in her eyes, I realized I'd missed my cue. A blunder I recovered quickly from as I turned and took both her hands in mine. I hadn't bothered to write anything out for the occasion; there hadn't been time. Besides, everything I needed to say was already in my heart.

"Lexi, our path hasn't always been a straight one," I began. "But everything on our journey has led us to where we are right now and I can't imagine having done it any other way. Today, I choose you to be my partner for the rest of my life. To love and support and stand by you through whatever else life has to throw at us. I've never felt a love deeper or purer than the love I feel for you and Ben. You complete me in every way." I reached into my pocket for the ring. I slid the simple band from the chapel onto her finger.

A single tear slipped down her cheek and I reached out to catch it, wiping it away gently.

"And Lexi," the officiant said. "Do you have something you'd like to share with Leo?"

She nodded and squeezed my hands. "We've come so far since that first day all those years ago when our lives changed forever and I want you to know that my heart has never been so full than it is today. I vow to honor you and cherish you and our family every day of my life. You are my love and my inspiration and..." She looked down at our hands. We waited a beat and soon she looked up, tears in her eyes, a smile on her face and she shook her head. "There just aren't the right words to express what we have, you know?"

I knew exactly what she was saying. The love we had, that we'd always shared. It defied explanation.

"I love you."

"I love you too, Leo."

Uncaring about the rest of the ceremony, I pulled her into my arms and kissed her deeply and passionately. From somewhere behind me, I heard the justice of the peace declare us husband and wife, but it was merely a formality.

~Lexi~

I COULD HAVE KISSED Leo forever. No. I could have kissed my *husband* forever.

I didn't realize exactly how much it would mean to have him declared officially my husband. But it was definitely a special feeling knowing that finally we were a family. Legally as well as spiritually.

The small group gathered as witnesses burst into cheers, but it was Ben tugging on my dress who finally forced me to pull away from Leo.

"Come on, Mom," he said. "That's gross. Seriously."

We laughed and bent down to include him in our hug.

I'd meant what I'd said: my heart had never been so full.

"What do you say," Leo whispered in my ear. "Should we get this party started?"

I nodded and linked my arm through Leo's. With Ben holding my other hand, we turned to start celebrating with our small group of friends both present and with us through videoconferencing.

"Congratulations, guys!" Keith hollered and let out a whoop.

"It's about time." Nicole's voice came through the speaker attached to her screen. "I'm so happy for you. Leo, give her a big juicy kiss for me." An order he happily carried out.

We spent the next few minutes making our rounds, including stops by the video screens to check in with Nicole and Enid, and I was so busy with the chaos of the moment that when I felt the first twinge in my belly, I wasn't sure that's what it was at all. The second pain was definitely that: a pain. I turned away from the group before I clutched my stomach. I didn't want anyone to see if there was nothing to see. I focused on a nearby candle flame and drew deep breaths, forcing myself to stay calm.

After a moment, the pain was gone and everything felt normal. I stretched and cautiously bent from side to side, but still...everything felt fine.

Lexi, you're just being paranoid. Cramps are a normal part of pregnancy. You're fine.

I'm fine.

I laughed at myself and my paranoia before I turned to rejoin the group. I was being ridiculous. As soon as I turned, my eyes met Leo's. He raised his eyebrow in question, his concern obvious. I flashed him the biggest and brightest smile I could. Everything was fine. No, it was better than fine. We were married, going to expand our family, and I truly couldn't be happier. I needed to stop worrying about things that hadn't happened and weren't going to happen.

No. Nothing was going to happen.

"Let's dance!" I called out on a whim. "I feel like dancing."

Right on cue, music started to play through the speakers, Chantal Kreviazuk's version of "It Feels Like Home." Leo took my hand, turned it and placed a kiss in my palm before wrapping it in his own and leading me to the middle of the marble floor. He swept me up in his arms, held me tight and moved me slowly around our makeshift dance floor. I tipped my head into his chest and inhaled deeply the scent that was uniquely my Leo.

"Are you happy?" he whispered as we twirled, my dress floating around my ankles.

I kissed his chest through the cotton of his shirt and looked up into his eyes. "I've never been happier." It was true; my heart felt about to burst. The day had been full of twists and emotional highs and lows, but ultimately, I had my family all together and more importantly, safe. And even more than that, I was Leo's wife. A detail I hadn't placed that much importance on in the past, but now that it was my reality, I couldn't imagine how we'd put it off for so long. "I'm your wife."

"You are."

"And you are my husband."

"That's true, too." He bent to kiss me on the cheek, but he missed because another cramp seized my belly and this time I couldn't hide it.

I released his hands and clutched my stomach; my teeth clenched together. I tried to slow my breath, to breathe through what was just a normal twinge of pregnancy, but the panic and what-ifs of what was actually happening threatened to overtake me.

"Lexi?"

I shook my head and squeezed my eyes tight. If I didn't look at him, if I didn't answer him, it wasn't real.

Leo's hands squeezed my upper arms in an effort to get me to respond.

When I felt the telltale wetness between my legs, the damp spot in my pretty, brand-new, white wedding underthings begin to spread...there was no other choice. It was real.

I tipped my head up and opened my eyes, seeing my own worry and pain reflected in his eyes. "Lexi?"

My name was loaded with unasked questions, but all I could do was say, "Something's wrong."

CHAPTER THIRTEEN

~Leo~

Something was wrong.

Something was very wrong.

The second she'd looked at me on the dance floor, I knew.

I had Lexi wrapped in a blanket, tucked tightly against my chest in the backseat of Keith's car as we drove dangerously fast toward the city of Las Vegas, and a hospital.

We careened around a corner. I looked up to meet Keith's eyes in the rearview mirror. "You okay back there?"

I nodded and he focused his attention back on the road.

"Lex? How are you doing?" I tipped her chin up so her eyes would meet mine. She was being brave, but I could see it in her face. She was terrified. And rightly so. We'd just allowed ourselves to think this baby would be okay. That everything would be fine.

And it still would.

I had to believe that.

"Everything will be okay, Lexi." I pulled her tighter against me. "I promise."

It was a promise both of us knew I might not be able to keep. But I'd make it anyway. Anything to make it better.

WE ARRIVED at the hospital in what had to be record time. I hopped out of the car, ran to Lexi's door and pulled it open. Before she could take a step out the door, I reached in and lifted her into my arms. The blanket slipped off, revealing her dress and the small red spot staining the gauzy, creamy fabric. My heart clenched in my chest and I had to swallow hard to keep my emotions under control.

Keith had run ahead and alerted the nurses in the emergency room that we were coming, so when I walked through the sliding doors with my wife in my arms, there was already a stretcher waiting for her.

I put her down as gently as I could, but wouldn't let go of her hand as the nurses wheeled her down the hall. My eyes held hers, trying in vain to comfort her in a situation where there was just no comfort to be had.

"We'll take it from here, sir."

The stretcher stopped in front of two steel doors marked Authorized Personnel Only but I wasn't about to let go of her hand. There was no way I was leaving her side. "I'm going with you."

"I'm sorry, sir," the nurse, who looked to be barely out of high school, responded. "It's hospital policy. You'll have to wait out here. There's a family—"

"No. I need to be with her."

"Sir. The sooner you comply, the sooner we can get your wife looked at. I'm sure you—"

"Leo." Lexi's voice was thin and strained. A tear slipped down her cheek. "It's okay."

"I'm not leaving you." I bent down so my face hovered over hers. "I can't leave you."

She forced a smile so heartbreakingly sad, it shattered me. "Everything will be okay," she said. "Didn't you just promise me that?"

I nodded.

"Then it will be."

I kissed her softly, gently on the lips, and stood, reluctantly releasing my grip on her hand. Her fingers trailed through mine as they wheeled her through the doors, and away from me.

~Lexi~

THE ROOM WAS a flurry of activity as the nurses asked me over and over how far along I was, if I'd had any cramping, any other symptoms of miscarriage.

Miscarriage.

That word resonated like a bell over and over in my head.

Yes.

Yes, I'd had other symptoms of miscarriage. The three other times I'd experienced one. Another fact I shared with the nurses.

"But this time?" the young, blonde nurse asked. "Have there been any other symptoms? Any cramps besides today?"

Wasn't today enough?

"Any bleeding? Besides now?"

Again. Isn't this enough? I wanted to scream, but I gritted my teeth and shook my head.

"Have you suffered any trauma? Any falls or—"

"No." I shook my head again. "Nothing. Everything has been fine. I haven't even been sick. A little nausea, and some tiredness, but..." I trailed off as I saw the nurses exchange looks. I knew what they were thinking. Morning sickness was a sign of a healthy pregnancy. To not have any...well, it was something I'd thought of a few times myself. "My doctor confirmed the pregnancy a few weeks ago," I told them.

No. I hadn't had an ultrasound.

No. I wasn't sure of my dates.

No. My periods hadn't been regular since the last miscarriage.

No. I hadn't heard the heartbeat.

No.

No.

NO!

I knew what they were saying. Or more specifically, not saying.

The older nurse, Connie, her name tag said, put her hand on my shoulder. "We're going to take your vitals and we'll get the doctor in here right away to check things out. Okay?"

I nodded.

There was no point asking whether everything was okay. I'd been through this before. *A threatened abortion,* one medical resident had called it the first time I'd miscarried. I would never forget her. Dr. Coffee. A suitable name for a resident, to be sure. She couldn't have been older than twenty-two or twenty-three and definitely had never had children of her own. It was clear that she had no idea the heartache her three little words had caused. Especially considering we had lost that baby. I'd never forgotten her or her lack of caring.

But these nurses weren't Dr. Coffee. They were kind and caring, and I could see the concern in their eyes as they ran their simple tests and took my vital signs. "Okay, Lexi," the young blonde nurse, Jenni, said. "I'm just going to go get the doctor. Try to take deep breaths, okay?"

I nodded. I'd try.

The doctor came quickly, much faster than I'd expected. Or maybe time no longer had any meaning. He was young, but not too young. Not that it mattered. He smiled kindly but it didn't do anything to calm my fears. I wondered where Leo was.

"Mrs. Mendez." The doctor addressed me and it took me a second to realize he was talking to me. I was married. I was Leo's wife, Mrs. Mendez. It seemed like a hundred years ago we'd said our vows to each other. "I'm Doctor Turner and I'm going to take care of you." I nodded. "Your vitals look good," he continued. "So we're going to go ahead and do a quick ultrasound to see what's going on, okay?" I nodded again. "There's nothing to worry about, Mrs. Mendez. So I need you to try to stay calm, okay?"

I looked at him and finally said what I was thinking. "How can I not worry?"

"I know it seems scary, but often times, cramps and bleeding are perfectly normal."

Often times. "And the other times?"

Doctor Turner looked at me, his lips pressed into a line. He didn't need to say anything; we both knew exactly what the other times meant. "Let's just get the ultrasound and see what we're dealing with. Sound good?"

I nodded. "My husband...can he..."

It was the young blonde nurse who answered. "I'm sorry, Mrs. Mendez. It's hospital policy to restrict visitors in the ER. It's just too busy. I'm sure you understand."

I nodded, although I most definitely didn't understand. Not at all.

"I'll tell you what." Connie wheeled a cart with an ultrasound monitor to the bedside. "I'll just run out to the waiting room and let him know that you're doing just fine. Okay?"

I nodded again and bit my lip to keep from screaming. Because it was a lie.

I wasn't fine.

Everything was far from fine.

~Leo~

THE ROOM WAS sixteen by sixteen.

Feet, that is.

My feet, more specifically. I knew because I'd paced the circumference of it at least fifty times since they'd shown me to the tiny family waiting room after taking Lexi away.

Why I couldn't go with her, I couldn't understand, but there was nothing to be gained by making a scene. Keith joined me after parking the car, but I sent him away again. I couldn't sit there and make small talk with anyone. Not when my wife was in distress.

My wife.

The word was still new and it made me sad to think that only a few hours ago we'd pronounced our love to each other and our family and now we were in the hospital awaiting the news that...no.

No.

I wouldn't think about it. I wouldn't let my mind go to the worst possible scenario.

I couldn't.

"Mr. Mendez?"

I whirled around to see a woman in scrubs in the doorway.

"Yes." I rushed to stand in front of her. "My wife. Is she...can I see her?"

"My name is Connie." She smiled kindly. "Your wife is just fine."

"So she's okay? The baby?"

Connie gave me a look that they must practice in nursing school: a noncommittal pursing of the lips that told me nothing at all. "We're just going to do a quick ultrasound to see what's going on and what might have been causing your wife's cramping."

"And the bleeding."

She nodded. "Yes."

"Can I be with her?"

Connie shook her head. "I'm afraid not, Mr. Mendez. It's against hospital policy, but I wanted to let you know what was happening. I should be getting back."

I reached my hand out to stop her, but stopped short of grabbing her. "Wait." I needed to know more. I needed to know something. She hadn't told me anything at all, but I couldn't formulate any words that made any sense or said what I needed them to say. I knew she was in a hurry. She had to be very busy, but to her credit she didn't rush me. "Will she...I mean...do you think she'll..." I couldn't finish the question. Tears pricked at the back of my eyes, but I blinked them back. I needed to hold it together.

Connie took my hand that still hung in the air and she squeezed in a way that was oddly comforting. "We're doing everything we can, Mr. Mendez. I promise to come and get you as soon as I can."

And then she was gone. I was alone in the tiny waiting room, which I suppose should have been a blessing. Instead, it suddenly felt empty. Lonely and cold.

I counted the steps to the closest chair. Four.

I sank into the hard molded plastic. I had no energy left to pace and count. I dropped my head into my hands.

"Leo?"

I lifted my head to see Keith in the space Connie had just vacated.

"I thought you could use one of these." He held out two cups of coffee. "And a friend."

I nodded. I'd never been happier to have someone ignore my request to be alone. "Thank you, Keith." I took the cup he handed me and popped the top.

Black. Just the way I needed it.

"I've never been married," Keith said after a moment. "And I don't have any kids. None of my own, anyway," he amended quickly. "But if you think it'll help to talk, I'm here to listen."

I nodded again. If he'd asked me when we'd first brought Lexi in and they'd whisked her away, I would have said no. But something about the nurse walking away, leaving me with more questions than anyone had answers for, had changed things.

I was silent for another moment and sipped at the hot brew. It was strong and bitter and absolutely perfect. "You know this will be the fourth time we've tried to have another baby?"

"No." Keith shook his head. "I didn't know."

"I thought we were going to quit trying," I continued. "I wanted to quit. I know how bad she wanted another baby, but I couldn't keep doing it. It's too hard. To watch the woman you love get her hopes raised and then subsequently destroyed in such a cruel fashion..." I shook my head. "It's too much. I couldn't do it anymore. Especially because I know she was doing it for me."

I swallowed hard, letting the words settle on the air. I'd never spoken the thought aloud. It tasted sour on my tongue.

"She did it for you?"

I nodded. "Lexi would never say so, but I know she felt guilty that I'd missed out on Ben's early years."

"Because of—"

"The whole not knowing I had a child thing," I finished for him with a wry grin. There was no bitterness about the past. Our lives had been star-crossed in the beginning, and fate, or maybe it was destiny, brought us back together, but neither of us dwelled on the lost time. "But it didn't matter."

"You didn't want another child?" Keith asked the question innocently enough, but for me it was loaded.

Of course I did. I wanted more than anything to see our family grow. To watch Lexi's body change with the life we created inside. I wanted to be that dad who got up in the middle of the night to get the baby and bring her back to her mother. I wanted to push a stroller, change diapers, hear her first word. All of it. Of course I wanted it.

But I wanted the family I already had even more. I wanted us whole and well and watching the way Lexi broke a little bit more with each lost pregnancy...it wasn't worth it. I told Keith as much.

He nodded as if he understood, but I know he didn't. How could he? I could only understand a fraction of the heartache that Lexi went through.

My heart squeezed in my chest and I forced myself to take another sip of the bitter coffee to keep focused. "I'm not doing it again." I shook my head. The thought came quickly with a ferocity I could hardly contain. But I knew it was right. "I won't do it. I won't put her through this again. After this time...no more." I jumped up from my chair again. Unable to sit still, I paced around the room again, counting steps as I went.

"You don't know how it's going to end, Leo."

It was true. I didn't. "Based on past history, I—"

"Leo." Keith stood and blocked my path. He was so close, I

could feel his breath as he stared me dead in the eye and repeated himself. "You don't know how it's going to end. Wait for the doctor to do his work."

"You don't under—"

"Wait." He straightened, boring into me with his gaze. "For the doctor. To do. His work."

I turned and slumped into a chair. The energy oozed from my body. "You're right."

"I know."

I shot Keith a look.

"Seriously," he said. "Just wait. There's no point in making plans or thinking about any scenarios until you know something. You'll only make yourself crazy."

He had a point. But there was one other point that popped into my head the moment Lexi was wheeled away from me in the strange hospital, surrounded by unfamiliar nurses and doctors. We should have been at home. In the mountains. With the doctor who knew her history, who had cared for her through all the other miscarriages. We should be closer to our friends who are like family.

I'd been selfish. I'd been wanting something that might not be the best thing for my family. The family I loved more than my own life. My own career.

I bit my lower lip and nodded. "You're right," I told Keith. "But even without knowing what's happening in there, I know one thing."

He looked at me and I could see in his eyes, he knew what I was going to say and he didn't want to hear it. But still, he listened as I said, "When all this is over, I'm taking my family home."

~Lexi~

"THIS IS GOING to be a bit cool." The doctor squirted the ultrasound gel on my exposed stomach, but I didn't even feel it. I was too focused on the ceiling above my stretcher. I traced the lines in the tiles, and blocked out the conversations of the nurses, the rhythmic beeping from somewhere behind my head, and the muffled noises beyond the curtain.

I closed my mind to all of it, focusing instead on talking to my guardian angel. Uncle Ray. After he died five years earlier, I liked to think of him as my angel, looking over me and guiding me through the hard times. It had been years since I'd actually *spoken* to him in any capacity, but at that moment, lying there all alone, I needed him. And I somehow knew he'd be there.

Uncle Ray. If you're listening. Please let my baby be okay. I bit my bottom lip to keep the tears back. *I know I've asked before, but this time it's different. I know this baby is supposed to be here, Uncle Ray. She's going to complete our family. Please hold her hand. Tell her to hang in there and be strong.*

Up until that moment, I hadn't thought of the baby as either a boy or a girl, but suddenly I knew with certainty.

"Okay," I heard the doctor say as he put the wand to my belly. "Let's see what's going on, shall we?"

I squeezed my eyes tighter and tried not to hold my breath.

Please, Uncle Ray.

"Okay," Dr. Turner said. "There's the head..."

Please.

"And the—wait."

Please, let her be okay. Please. It has to—

"Lexi?" Jenni, the blonde nurse who stood by my head, squeezed my shoulder. "Lexi?" She said my name again.

I opened my eyes, and focused on her and the cartoon

bunnies on her scrubs. "Yes." I blinked hard. "Is she...is she okay?"

Jenni's smile was bright. "She feels like a girl, does she?"

I nodded. Yes, she was definitely a girl.

"Mrs. Mendez." Dr. Turner moved the wand around some more, occasionally stopping to push buttons on the keyboard. "Judging by the dates you gave, you estimate to be around thirteen weeks?"

"Yes."

"And did you say that this is your first ultrasound?"

I nodded and then said again, "Yes. We were going to schedule one for when I got back to Canada."

"Hmm..."

Hmm? What the hell did that mean?

I struggled to try to sit up but I couldn't see the screen. Not that I would have been able to decipher anything anyway. I'd had enough ultrasounds to know they were almost impossible to read for the untrained eye. Still, I tried.

"Lexi." Jenni's hands were on my shoulders, pressing me gently back into the table. "You have to lie still so the doctor can do his job. We're almost done."

I did as I was told, but craned my neck around so I could see the nurse's face. Tears slipped from my eyes, but I didn't move to wipe them away. I wanted to ask again whether she was okay, but I bit my lip. I knew enough to know that if they weren't telling me, there was nothing positive to say.

~Leo~

WITH THE COFFEE Keith had brought me long gone, I'd taken to pacing the waiting room again, and had made another dozen laps when the same nurse, Connie, who'd come to talk to me before, appeared in the door again.

"Mr. Mendez?"

I moved so quickly, I almost knocked her over in my haste. "Is she okay? What's happening?"

Connie smiled. "I can take you back now."

"Is she okay?" I asked again. "The baby? Is the baby okay?"

"Come with me, Mr. Mendez." She turned and I followed, trying not to step on her heels as I went. "She's still in the ER, so you'll have to calm down and try to be quiet." She turned to look at me. "I'm actually bending the rules a little bit in this case, so please don't make me regret it."

I nodded and swallowed hard. I would be strong. I had to be strong for Lexi. She was the one who needed me. She'd be hurting and I knew just how to handle it.

I followed her through two big double doors, and instantly the atmosphere changed. The eerie quiet of the hallway and waiting room morphed into a frenzied charge, filling the air around us. Myriad voices, beeping, and sounds I couldn't quite identify filled the air. If they'd been worried about me causing any kind of disturbance with my presence, I couldn't figure out how it would have made any difference.

"She's just in here." Connie pulled back a curtain to reveal Lexi tucked into a hospital bed. She had an IV in one hand and a monitor on a finger of the opposite hand. She looked impossibly tiny. Even with her swollen belly, which I swore had practically doubled in size in the few days we'd been in Las Vegas. "You can go to her," Connie said, snapping me out of the trance I was in.

Lexi turned at the sound of the nurse's voice. "Leo." Her eyes filled with tears, jarring me into action. I rushed to her bedside, cupped her cheeks in my hands and planted a small flurry of kisses all over her face. If I could, I'd kiss away her pain.

I'd kiss away all the hurt and take her out of here and we'd go home where we could heal. Together.

"I'm so sorry, baby." I could feel her warm tears against my skin as I pressed my face to hers. I needed to feel her, have her close to me. "It's okay," I murmured. "It will all be okay." I pulled back just enough so I could see her eyes. Tears flowed freely from their beautiful green depths. My chest ached to see the pain my love was going through. I moved my hands down to hers and held them tight, never taking my eyes off hers. "Lex, we'll get through this and we'll be okay. Stronger. And I don't want to try anymore. Not if it means this. We have Ben. He's healthy and perfect and the two of you are all I'll ever need." She shook her head slightly and opened her mouth to speak, but I kissed her softly before I continued. I needed to say everything I'd been thinking while I waited in that room. "And we're not staying here," I said. "This isn't home. The lake is home. The lake, the cabin, and the inn. As soon as I can, I'm taking you home, Lex."

"Lexi?" I swung my head around to see a young blonde nurse I hadn't noticed before. She smiled as if our whole world hadn't just shattered. Again. I narrowed my eyes and would have left Lexi's side to physically remove her from the room if it hadn't been for her next words. "You should probably tell him, Lexi."

I looked back to my wife, her face an unreadable mix of emotion. "Lexi?" I said her name slowly. "Tell me what?"

~Lexi~

I ALMOST LAUGHED at the look on Leo's face, but not because it was funny. But more because I couldn't process what had just transpired in the last few minutes. I was still processing everything the doctor had told me when Leo came in and I was just so happy to see him and have him near me, holding me, kissing me. Having him there made everything better and oh, so real.

"Lexi?" He said my name again. "Tell me what?" It was the second time he'd asked. I swallowed hard and struggled to find the words. He looked behind him again to Jenni. "What's going on?" he demanded of her. "Someone better tell me. And soon."

"Leo." I reached for him and pulled his gaze back to me. "It's okay."

"What's okay?" He shook his head. I could see where his mind was at. That much was obvious, even if he hadn't just given me a super sweet speech about how everything was going to be okay.

I couldn't help it; fresh tears slipped down my cheeks. "Leo," I managed. "We didn't lose the baby."

"Lexi, I said that—wait. What?" I could see the questions cross his face rapidly as he tried to process what I'd just said. "We didn't lose the baby?"

"No." I smiled, and quickly added, "Either of them."

"We didn't..." He looked from me, to the nurse, back to me. His eyes were wide, questioning, but it took a moment for the other part of what I'd said to sink in. "What did you...did you just say..."

I nodded. Fresh tears filled my eyes. It was impossible to think I could still cry, but these tears were born purely of joy. "Twins."

"What?" Leo put his hands on my stomach, moving the sheet out of the way so he could touch bare skin. His hands were gentle, only featherlight as they skimmed the surface of my stomach. "Twins?" He looked up into my eyes and I nodded. "And they're...they're okay?"

I nodded again, remembering what the doctor had said.

"Hмм..." Dr. Turner had clucked his tongue and moved the wand over my belly and I'd wanted to jump up, grab him by the coat and demand to know what was going on. Instead, I'd settled back into the bed and he'd continued to move the wand, typing things into his computer and finally, after what had felt like forever, he said, "Do you know there were two in there?"

"Pardon?" *Two?* I propped myself up on my elbows and stared at him.

"Twins, Mrs. Mendez." He smiled. "Congratulations, you're expecting twins."

"And are they..." I didn't want to finish the question, but the bleeding and the cramping was still fresh in my mind. I hadn't made it up; I knew it was bad...I had to know. "Are they okay?"

Doctor Turner's smile said it all. "They look fine. Two strong heartbeats and their legs are kicking like crazy."

"But the bleeding. The cramping."

His mouth pressed into a line, but he nodded reassuringly. "Sometimes that happens and as scary as it can be, it's perfectly normal. In your case, it appears as if the placenta is sitting quite low in your uterus, which may be why there was some blood present. Quite honestly, bleeding is quite common and most of the time we never know exactly why it happens. The important thing to know is that your babies look strong and healthy."

Strong and healthy. The words played on repeat in my mind. They were the only words that mattered.

"And by the look of your placenta, I'd say they were identical twins."

"Identical?"

He smiled. "Identical girls from what I can see here."

. . .

Now, with Leo holding my hand, I told him everything the doctor had said. Jenni helped by filling in the blanks of the story that I couldn't remember or was too emotional to repeat. I finished with the word *identical* and Leo stared at me, slack-jawed.

"Twins?"

I nodded.

"Really?"

I nodded again.

"And they're okay?"

"Yes." The smile on my face was so big it almost hurt, but I was never going to quit smiling. Ever.

He let out a whoop and pulled me into his arms, hugging me tight before he let go just as quickly. "Oh, I'm sorry," he said. "I should be careful."

"I'm not going to break, Leo."

He looked at Jenni, who shook her head. "She's not going to break. In fact, Dr. Turner says that everything looks great. He wants you to follow up with your doctor at home. Usually twin pregnancies are considered high risk, and with Lexi's past history, I think it would be prudent to be a little more cautious than usual, but really, Dr. Turner agrees, there's no real reason to be concerned here."

Leo looked at me and smiled. "That's great news." He cupped my face in his hands and kissed me. I vaguely heard the nurse as she excused herself from the room and then we were alone with the news that not only was our baby okay, but our *babies* were okay.

When he'd recovered enough from the shock of the news, Leo pulled up a chair and sat next to my bed, one hand in mine, the other on my belly. We sat that way for a few minutes in silence, simply absorbing everything that had happened in the last twenty-four hours.

The silence was soon broken when Nurse Connie poked her head in the curtain. I clutched my hand tighter to Leo's. I wasn't going to let him leave. I knew they were bending the rules by letting him in there with me. But I wasn't going to let him leave my side. Not after everything I'd just been through on my own.

"Please don't make him go."

Connie smiled. "Don't you worry, he can stay," she said. "In fact...I ran into a little man in the waiting room who'd really like to make sure his mom's doing okay."

Just then Ben pushed past her, through the curtain and ran to my bedside. I caught him in my arms as much as I could and Leo lifted him so he was perched on the edge of the bed.

"Thank you." I mouthed the words over Ben's head to Connie.

"I'll give you guys a minute, okay?"

"Are you okay, Mom?" Ben's eyes were so full of concern, it cracked my heart a little bit to see my sweet boy so full of worry. "Roxanne told me not to worry, but you're in the hospital and when Uncle Ray went to the—"

"It's nothing like Uncle Ray." I hadn't even thought of that. The last time Ben had been in a hospital was to visit the man who was like his grandfather. Right before he passed away. I held Ben a little tighter. "I'm perfectly fine," I mumbled into his head. "I promise, it's nothing like Uncle Ray, okay?"

He nodded but I could tell he wasn't convinced.

"In fact, your mother and I have something to tell you."

Ben turned to look at his father. "Is it the baby?" His face was a solemn mask, his need to be a strong little man heartbreakingly sweet.

"It is about the baby," Leo said, just as serious. He glanced at me and I tried not to give him away with a smile. "In fact," Leo looked back at Ben, "I have some very important news about the baby and her sister."

"Sister?" Ben shook his head and looked back to me. "But I'm the baby's brother."

"You are," I assured him. "But the baby," I took his hand and put it on my stomach, "also has a twin sister. You're going to be a big brother to twins."

I could see the wheels turning in Ben's head as he looked between us. Finally he spoke. "Twins? Like, two of them?"

"Yes," Leo answered. "Two."

"Two girls?"

Leo nodded, still serious. "Identical girls."

"Like, *two* sisters?" He looked to me for clarification. I raised my eyebrows and nodded in agreement. "Whoa." Ben shook his head and looked back to his dad. "We're going to be totally outnumbered."

For the next few minutes, we chatted and I caught Ben up with what the doctor had said, reassuring him that the babies were indeed fine. As we talked, he snuggled next to me on the small bed and pretty soon his eyes drifted shut. I looked to the clock over the door. It was after midnight. Ben's birthday.

"It's been a crazy day, hasn't it?" I extended my arm to Leo. He wrapped his fingers through mine.

"You could say that, *Mrs. Mendez*."

I lifted my left hand so I could see the ring he'd slid on my finger a few hours earlier. I hadn't taken time to look at it closely. It was a simple silver band that looked vaguely familiar. He saw me looking and traced the ring with his hand. "I know it isn't much," he said. "It's from the chapel."

I swallowed a laugh. "Part of the Cherish the Moment package?"

"Exactly. I knew it would come in handy. But it's only temporary. I'll get you a new one. A better one."

"No." I shook my head. "It's perfect."

"It'll turn your finger green."

"I love it and everything it represents. It's so Vegas. It's so...us." I looked into his eyes, suddenly overcome by how far we'd come from that first night all those years ago when we'd danced until our feet hurt and ate greasy burgers in a diner. The night Ben was conceived. And of course, all the years in between that led me back to Vegas and to Leo. Fate, or was it the city that had brought us back together again? Some people thought of Las Vegas as Sin City. Something to be feared, shunned, or at the very least, held to some type of sordid standard. Heck, for years I'd avoided it myself. Convinced it was a terrible place where only bad things happened despite all the good there'd been. But it wasn't bad. How could it be?

I closed my eyes and drew in a deep breath. In that moment with my husband and son, our unborn twins, healthy and tucked safely in my belly, I'd never felt more at peace and I knew what I needed to do.

"Leo? What you said earlier...about going back to Canada." He nodded, but I shook my head. "No," I said simply. He opened his mouth, but I wouldn't give him a chance to say anything. "We're staying here. Oasis is here and it's such a good opportunity."

"Lexi, I—"

"But it's not just that." The thoughts had been forming in my head almost from the moment we'd landed in Vegas, but it was only now that everything had become clear and I'd never felt more certain of anything in my life. "It's everything," I continued. "Look at our history."

"That's exactly what I'm doing," Leo said. "And that's why I'm going to take you home."

"But don't you see." I shook my head slightly. "We already *are* home."

His mouth opened but nothing came out and he closed it again. His head tipped down so I couldn't see his eyes. I waited him out and when he finally looked up, I could see his decision had been made, too. He placed a kiss on the back of my hand before he rose from his chair. He moved first to Ben, kissing him softly on his forehead, and then to my sheeted belly, which he kissed twice before his lips met mine in a slow, gentle kiss. When he pulled away, our eyes connected. "You're right," he said quietly, his voice choking on emotion. "We *are* home."

EPILOGUE

May

~Lexi~

They were cherubic. At least for the moment. I'd take it.

I'd never known such exhaustion. Even when Ben was a baby. It was nothing like having two of them. But I wouldn't change it for anything.

There'd be time to sleep later. Much later, if the beginning was any indication. I glanced down at their sleeping forms tucked into their bassinets with little more than cotton receiving blankets over them because of the Nevada heat that was already starting to permeate the spring morning.

The stone patio of our suite, overlooking the desert gardens that had begun to thrive with the careful tending of the new groundskeeper, had become one of my favorite places to sit when the twins were sleeping. Which admittedly wasn't as often as I'd like. But they were only a few weeks old. That would come with time, too.

I didn't hear him come up behind me, but I felt my husband's presence before he kissed me on the top of my head. "Good morning, sexy mama."

"Hardly." I laughed. It had been at least two days since I'd washed my hair, and my belly was still saggy and lumpy after being stretched out so completely by two little humans, but when Leo looked at me, all he saw was beauty and I believed him.

"I didn't hear you get up with them this time." He moved around me, bending to kiss both Hannah and Sophie on their chubby cheeks before he sat next to me. "You should have woken me. I would have—"

"You were exhausted." I squeezed his hand. It was true. Leo had been working overtime since the busy spring season had started. After the soft launch at Christmas, we'd opened officially at New Years and despite a few tiny glitches, the Oasis had become an instant success. With the target guest aimed at families, and armed with a variety of family-friendly activities that Roxanne and I had developed, it hadn't taken long for the resort to start filling up with bookings. "How are the numbers looking these days?"

"Fantastic." Leo handed me a cup of tea from the tray Joanne had brought up. The staff was taking very good care of me since I'd brought the twins home three weeks ago, making sure I never wanted for anything while I got used to being the mother of not only a busy twelve year old but two very demanding newborns as well. "We should be eighty percent full next weekend. And if things continue to grow, we'll be full this summer. I can hardly believe how well it's going."

"I can believe it." I leaned over to kiss him. "You've worked so hard. You guys deserve this."

"No." He held my left hand, tracing my still swollen fingers with his own. "We all have. I could never have done this without you, Lex."

My heart swelled and tears pricked at my eyes. Since the babies were born, my emotions were even more out of control, but I knew they'd settle out. Everything would. Leo reached out and cupped my cheek before kissing me softly. "I love you, Lexi. You are—"

One of the babies let out a small cry. A cry I'd come to recognize as the precursor for a much louder one if she didn't get picked up immediately. Hannah was definitely our feisty baby. "Hold that thought." I smiled at the interruption and bent to pick up the baby. She fit perfectly in my arms, and I bounced her gently. As I watched, her tiny face settled from the scowl back into contentment, without her eyes even opening.

"You're amazing," Leo said. "I mean, I've always thought you were an amazing mother, but to watch you with the babies." He shook his head in wonderment. "You're just incredible."

Right on cue, and the way I knew she would because she was so in sync with her sister, Sophie let out a cry. "Your turn, Daddy."

Without even the slightest hesitation, Leo bent to pick up his other daughter and tucked her protectively into the crook of his arm. He was a natural and Sophie quieted instantly. I watched him watching her for a few moments. Leo had always been the most attractive man in the world, and if someone had told me that I could ever love him more, or think him even more handsome, I would have told them it was impossible. Now I knew that it was true. Watching him with our girls, my love for him had only doubled.

"Hey."

I turned to see Ben, hair messed, standing in the door, rubbing sleep from his eyes. "Good morning, buddy."

He came and gave me a gentle hug since I was still holding Hannah. "Can I hold her?"

"Of course." Ben had proved to be a fantastic big brother and although his attentions were limited the way a twelve-year-old boy's were apt to be, he enjoyed helping out and it was easy to see the love he had for his little sisters as well. He was going to be a fantastic big brother as the years went on.

He settled into a chair next to Leo and I handed him the little pink bundle. Side by side, watching my boys holding my girls, I could no longer hold in my tears. They slipped down my cheeks and I didn't bother to wipe them away.

~Leo~

I HATED LEAVING my little family to go to work, even if it was only a two-minute walk to the main building. But there was work to be done, and I couldn't leave Keith to do it all, especially considering he was planning a wedding. I still laughed when I thought about how after two years of being together, it took Lexi and me getting married for Keith to finally pop the question to Roxanne.

They'd made their engagement official about a week after our dramatic nuptials, and the date was set for June first. The way Roxanne was talking, it was going to be much larger than ours had been, but she seemed to thrive on organizing events, which was also why I was going to talk to Keith about adding weddings to our list of offerings for Oasis. His new bride would be the perfect choice to oversee things.

I worked all morning, handling small issues that inevitably

came up overnight and before I knew it, it was time for lunch. Since they'd come home from the hospital, I'd joined Lexi, the babies, and occasionally Ben if he wasn't at school or playing in the pool, back at the suite for lunch. But Lexi told me she wanted to get out and take the babies for a bit of a walk today and would meet me at the restaurant for a lunch out. It wasn't far, but I knew getting two little humans organized would be a big effort, even for lunch. There was no way I was going to disagree. My wife could handle anything. I knew that now more than ever before.

I pushed my chair back from my desk, but before I could even get out the door, my phone rang again. I grabbed it without looking at the caller ID.

"Leo Mendez."

"Leo!" Nicole's voice hollered through the line and I shook my head with a smile.

"Hey, Nic. Were you trying to reach Lexi? This is my—"

"I know it's your number. I didn't want to bug her," she said hurriedly. "Besides, that's why I'm calling."

"Because you're—"

"We're coming to visit," she said before I could even get a word in. "Next week. Is there room?"

I laughed. "Of course there's room. Why so—"

"I need to see those babies and snuggle them. Besides, it's been way too long since little Jasper has seen his godparents. He's crawling now and it's not the same to experience those things over FaceTime."

That was the truth. After Lexi was cleared for travel, we'd gone back to Canada long enough for her to sort out her classroom and get her replacement settled, while I set Seth up properly at the inn. We'd packed and winterized the cabin and of course said our good-byes to our friends. It had been a quick visit, and we'd only been able to visit with Nicole, Ryan, and their newborn son, Jasper, for a few days. She was absolutely right; we were all long overdue for a visit.

"You're right, Nic. We'd love to see you and of course there's room. I'll set you guys up in a family suite. When are you coming?"

She gave me the final details of the flights she'd already booked, and I made some notes so I could send a car for them when they arrived. Lexi would be thrilled to have them here. I knew she wanted to go back to Lake Lillian for the summer, and we would. But not this summer. Not with the twins so brand new.

With Nicole still gabbing in my ear about the trip, I made my way down the hall and across the foyer of the main reception, which was now bustling with people. A marked change from only a few months ago. I stopped just outside the restaurant to finish my conversation. Through the glass, I could see everyone had gathered. Keith was already there with Roxanne and the kids. Lexi held center court with one of the twins in her arms. Roxanne held the other. It was impossible to tell them apart from a distance; heck, even from up close, I struggled. Ben, Evan, and Ruby were drinking bottles of soda and laughing about something. The whole scene made me happier than I'd ever thought possible.

"One more thing, Leo."

I focused my attention back to Nicole and what she was saying. "What's that?"

"Don't tell Lexi," she said. "Let's keep it a secret, okay?"

I let her words roll around in my head for a second, but only a second before I shook my head. "Sorry, Nicole. I don't keep secrets from my wife." *Not any more*, I added silently. *Not ever again.*

After finally begging off the call with Nicole, I took one more moment to watch my family through the glass before I pulled open the door and joined them in the restaurant. Lexi turned, her eyes meeting mine; her face lit up in a smile.

Watching her body transform over the last few months, and seeing the strength in her with the twins, she'd only become more beautiful. I'd loved every moment of seeing her belly grow, the little feet and hand prints that pressed against her skin. I'd sung to the girls while I rubbed their mama's feet. The last six months had passed in a whirlwind, and now that they were here, and the five of us were finally together, I knew without a doubt. It didn't matter whether we were in the Canadian mountains or Las Vegas—wherever Lexi and these three amazing kids were, as long as we were together, we would always be home.

I hope you enjoyed Lexi and Leo's journey to Vegas and back again.

If you are looking for some more love in the beautiful Rocky Mountains, you will absolutely fall for the McCormick brothers of Cedar Springs! You can one click Love in the Moment for free NOW! And read a special excerpt right after this!

And if you want even more romance...click <u>HERE</u> for an exclusive FREE novella that isn't available anywhere else!

LOVE IN THE MOMENT

Please enjoy this excerpt from the first in The McCormicks Series—Love in the Moment

Ian McCormick stole a glance at the woman sitting next to him. He'd picked her up only ten minutes earlier from the bus station and already he'd run out of things to talk about. In fact, beyond the general introductions they'd exchanged, they really hadn't spoken at all. He felt as if he should say something to break the silence, but every time he opened his mouth, he drew a blank. What was he supposed to say to the younger half-sister he'd never met?

The sister that he'd never had any desire to meet, not since finding out about her existence almost ten years ago. As far as he was concerned, Ian could have gone the rest of his life without knowing about Chelsea or her sister, Amber's existence. And he really didn't see any need to get to know either of them. After all, they were the reason his entire life had imploded all those years ago.

Okay, that wasn't entirely fair. It wasn't their fault that their father had led a secret life, with a completely different family. A family he'd finally left his *other* family for, leaving Ian, his brothers, and his mother all alone. *No. It wasn't the girls' fault.* But all of the reasoning in the world hadn't made it any easier for Ian to wrap his head around it. Despite the fact that it had been almost a decade ago.

He snuck another look at the girl who had barely looked up from her phone since she'd sat down in the jeep. There was definitely a family resemblance. She had their father's green eyes, just like he did. And the dark, thick hair. He hated to admit it, but there was no denying she was his sister. And it wasn't as if he could spend the whole summer not talking to her. He'd made a promise to Declan, his second youngest brother.

"*It's not her fault,*" Declan had said on the phone. "*Chelsea and Amber aren't to blame, Ian. You need to get over it.*"

Dec was right. He did need to get over it, especially since she was going to be staying with him all summer. He took a breath and opened his mouth to say something, but didn't have a chance.

"I know you hate me."

Ian shut his mouth dumbly.

"And I suppose you think you have a reason to," Chelsea continued. "But it wasn't my idea to come here, you know? Declan pretty much insisted that it would be *good for me* or something, and...well...I kinda trust Dec. Besides, I didn't really have anywhere else to go."

He swallowed hard, giving himself a moment. "I don't hate you." As he spoke the words, he realized they were true. "I just don't know you. And Declan's right. It will be good for you here."

"You don't even know why he said that."

"I don't need to." Ian slowed the jeep to take the turn that would lead them out of town, toward the cottages. His house sat at the end of a row of other log cabins that were used primarily by summer people. Most of the houses were built by families who came from the city for the summer months, and they were still locked up tight because the season wouldn't start for another month or so. It was quiet, but Ian liked it. At least for now, while he was getting settled. And it was true, he didn't know why Declan thought it was a good idea for Chelsea to get out of the city for the summer, but he had a few guesses, and there was no doubt that a little bit of quiet would be good for her, too. "I trust Declan, too," he said as the jeep bumped over the dirt road. It was impossible not to trust Declan. Out of all of his siblings, Dec was definitely the most trustworthy, and the most compassionate and caring and...he was pretty much everything good in the world. "If he thinks it'll be good for you out here, he's probably right."

She shrugged and turned back to her cell phone, looking up a moment later in horror. "The service is terrible here."

"One of my favorite features." He smiled.

"Why would that be a good thing?"

He ignored the question. "It's not that bad, really. Just a little spotty sometimes. Besides, you'll be able to get Wi-Fi at the Dockside as soon as I get it hooked up."

"The Dockside?"

"The new marina." Ian couldn't help but smile. "Cool name, right?" The main reason he'd returned to Cedar Springs was because the economy was starting to pick up, and there were business opportunities to be had. One of the first he'd found was the old marina. It was just next to the Grizzly Paw on the beach in town and Ian remembered it as *the* meeting place for summer fun. He picked it up for a bargain basement price, probably because it needed so much work. By the looks of things, it had sat empty for years and it would definitely take a little elbow grease to get it up and running again. Not that Ian was afraid of hard work. In fact, that had always been his favorite part of a new business: turning nothing into something. "I just closed on it yesterday. And with any luck, it will be open and ready for business in time for the season to start. But if that's going to happen, I'm going to need a little help."

She looked at him sideways. "And I suppose you want me to help."

"You got it. Call it...the price of admission."

She rolled her eyes and shoved her phone into her duffel bag. "Why not? I guess a summer job won't hurt."

"Oh no." Ian braced himself for her response to what he was about to tell her. "Helping at the marina isn't a summer job—it's just an expectation. I got you a job, too. You'll be starting at the Grizzly Paw right away. Sam's an old friend of mine, and she's doing me a favor by giving you this job, so I know you won't let me down."

"Two jobs?"

"No." He shook his head. "Just one. And a family project."

"But I'm never going to have any time to have fun," she wailed.

That was the point, at least as far as Ian was concerned. He didn't know much about twenty-two-year-old girls, but from what Declan had told him, Chelsea was making far too many poor choices. And as the big brother—whether he wanted to be or not—it was going to be his job to help her make good ones. Or keep her too busy to make anything but.

When Gwen Henderson had dreamed of her triumphant return to Cedar Springs after years of hard work and sacrifice, she'd dreamed of driving an expensive convertible down Main Street, her dark hair floating in the breeze as all the men's heads turned to see the beautiful and famous celebrity she'd turned out to be as they kicked themselves for not dating her when they had their chance.

Yes, in her fantasies, it was perfect. In reality, however, she had not imagined that on the eve of her summer visit to Cedar Springs, her secondhand Mustang would have some random, and likely expensive, engine problem that would require her taking the bus into town. And she most certainly did not expect that the one man who'd not only turned her down as a teenager, but had publicly humiliated her ten years earlier at the Summer Equinox Festival, would be there when she got off the bus.

Ian McCormick.

He didn't even *live* in Cedar Springs. What were the odds the one man who still haunted—no, not haunted...*visited*—her dreams would not only be standing there when she got off the stupid, humiliating bus, but would also look her square in the eye and not even recognize her?

If she was honest with herself, and she'd made that a habit over the last few years, that was the part that hurt the most. Ian McCormick had been her biggest teenage crush. No, her *only* teenage crush. Every summer for four years, she had lusted after him. Practically threw herself at him that final summer. But he'd barely even noticed her and when she thought she'd finally had a date with him at the festival, he'd stood her up. Left her there all alone. She knew now he'd only said yes to the date out of pity. After all, it didn't make sense for someone as handsome and smart as Ian McCormick to go out with fat, pimple-faced, four-eyed, frizzy-haired *Giant Gigi*. At the time, she'd been heartbroken—totally destroyed, really. But time and distance had taught her social order. The other thing time and distance had taught her was the impact that health, fitness, contacts, clear skin, a new hair-do, and a name change could do for social order.

It had been five years since she'd dropped the stupid childhood nickname, adopted a fitness regime and lost seventy-five pounds, finding herself and a new career in the process. Early on in her transformation, Gwen decided to document everything on social media, using a blog and then a Facebook and Instagram account to chronicle her progress. The result was not only a whole new body, but also a very loyal following, commercial and marketing deals, and the potential for a book and maybe even a reality television show. She was a very different person than the sad, overweight teenager she'd been on her summer visits to see her grandma in Cedar Springs. *Very* different. And with women looking up to her and men lining up to date her, she no longer needed Ian McCormick to validate her worth.

But if that was true, why had her heart done a stupid little flip when he'd grabbed her bag at the bus stop? And why had her pulse raced out of control when he looked at her? How was it even possible that he could still have that effect on her after all these years?

"Gwen!"

Deanna Gordon shot out of the building across the street and without even looking, raced across the street and pulled her into a hug. "Oh my goodness, you look amazing." Deanna held her out at arm's length for a fraction of a second before she pulled her back into a hug. "I'm so glad you're finally here. I was going to meet you at the bus stop—that's crazy that your car broke down—but I got caught up with a patient and—"

"It's okay." Gwen finally cut her off with a laugh. "I literally only walked half a block. Don't worry about it."

Deanna bent down and scooped up her bag. "Is this all you have? One duffel bag? I don't think I could travel that light if I tried."

Gwen laughed again. "Are you kidding? The rest of my bags are coming later. I may have sweet-talked the guy at the depot to deliver them personally."

"You did not?"

She only smiled in response. It wasn't often that Gwen used her curves and killer smile to get her way, but sometimes she couldn't seem to help herself. Besides, it's not as though she did it very often.

Deanna shook her head, but her friend smiled. "Hey, if you can get away with it...why not, right?"

"Exactly. And heaven knows I haven't always had this skill. I might as well take advantage sometimes. But don't tell anyone, okay?"

Deanna stared at her. "Who would I tell?"

She forgot sometimes that not everyone lived their whole life online. For Gwen, it was normal to record everything, and censor anything she didn't want getting out. It was a carefully constructed existence, one that was almost entirely public, because she'd built her following by *not* keeping very much private. Her readers liked to hear everything about her, including her workouts, what she had for dinner, her dates, and even more personal things about her dating habits. Not that she'd had much to report lately. She may get a lot of attention from men, but that attention disappeared pretty quickly when they found out who she was and what she did for a living.

"Forget it." Gwen shrugged it off. "I didn't really mean it like that. I mean..."

"I keep forgetting what you do for a living," Deanna said. "I mean, it's crazy to me that you can do that for a *job*. Oh, but I didn't mean it like that. I'm sorry, Gwen. It's just—"

"It's fine. I totally get it. It is crazy. I'm not offended." She decided to change tact and confide in the one person who would totally understand. "But you know what *did* offend me?"

Her friend froze on the sidewalk and waited.

"Ian McCormick." She pronounced every syllable of his name with an edge.

"Ian? You saw him?"

"You know he's here?"

Deanna blinked at her mildly before she put a smile back on her face and ushered Gwen down the sidewalk. "You know what? Let's drop your bag off and then you can tell me all about it over a cup of coffee."

Gwen eyed her friend and shook her head. "How about a *drink*?"

"Why didn't you tell me Ian McCormick was here?" Gwen sat across from Deanna at her kitchen table, a glass of soda water in her hand. She'd gone for the soda, deciding against alcohol. It was her default drink, but now that she had it, she wished she'd gone for something stronger after all. *Ian McCormick was in Cedar Springs.* That had not been part of the plan. Not at all. Sure, whenever she thought of her summers in Cedar Springs visiting her grandma, Ian figured largely in her memory. Whether he knew it or not, his attention—or lack thereof, as was the case—had figured largely in her teenage life. She couldn't remember a summer she hadn't spent lusting after him. As one of the *summer* kids, he was kind of a celebrity among the local kids. Not that she'd been a local kid. But she also wasn't a summer kid. Gwen had definitely floated and never really had any friends except for Deanna.

Ian had no shortage of girls after him, but he'd never wanted to date any of them.

No. That wasn't true. He just hadn't wanted to date *her*. Not that she could blame him. If she'd been a teenage boy back then, *she* wouldn't have wanted to date her. Almost a hundred pounds overweight, with bad hair and glasses, she was a walking cliché. Hell, she was even more of a cliché now that she'd lost all the weight, turned her life around and was returning to her past childhood haunts. She was a made-for-TV movie, for goodness sake.

"I honestly didn't think it mattered." Deanna joined her at the table. "He's a summer kid."

"A...he's not a kid anymore. And, B...you know he's way more than that. He's *way more*."

Deanna almost spat out her water. "No."

"No what?"

"No way you still have a thing for Ian McCormick."

Gwen didn't even have to answer that question, because the woman she'd always considered to be her best friend knew her well enough to know the answer. Or, she should have known her better than that, anyway. She narrowed her eyes and tilted her head.

"No way." Deanna shook her head. "Gwen, how can you possibly still be hung up on him? Honestly, I thought maybe after...well..."

"We said we'd never talk about that, remember?"

The situation they were never to discuss was a moment that could have broken up their friendship forever, but the girls made a decision not to let it affect them. Even though it had been hard, very hard for Gwen. The last summer she'd come to visit, Ian had arrived earlier than he usually had and somehow, Deanna and Ian ended up together at a party where they drank too much and...Gwen didn't like to think about it, but Deanna lost her virginity to Ian McCormick. She could have let it destroy their friendship, but Deanna felt terribly about it and she swore she'd never been more than just a friend with Ian and that's all it would ever be.

"Still," Deanna said. "I honestly didn't think you'd still be thinking of him at all."

How could she not? When they were kids, he'd actually

been nice to her. He even talked to her and the conversations they had were real. Not about stupid stuff where she had to pretend to be interested in whatever football team was going to the playoffs or who got drunk at whatever party. But real stuff like what they hoped to achieve with their lives, what the future looked like and where they wanted to go to college. And besides that, he'd been so gorgeous. Correction, he *was* gorgeous. Maybe even more so, if that was possible.

But he still doesn't know you're alive, Gwen, the little voice in her head reminded her. She wasn't more than a townie friend back then, and she was even less now.

"So, he didn't recognize you?" Deanna changed tack. "Not that I'm surprised. You look like a totally different person. Seriously, if I didn't know better, I wouldn't even recognize you and we've been friends since...well, forever. You look crazy good."

Gwen blushed and waved away the compliment. She couldn't seem to get used to the attention she got from people who knew her *when.* It was almost easier for people to think she was just naturally thin and fit. Except when it came to her blog. But talking about her experiences online was a totally different thing. It was safe to hide behind the screen.

In fact, throughout her transformation, it had been a sort of therapy almost. Her website was the place she went to decompress and work through all the feelings that went along with her journey.

She should blog about Ian. Why hadn't she thought of that earlier? It made perfect sense. She could have a chance to process her feelings about seeing him again. *And still being invisible.* And she'd already made her summer vacation into an *event.* When she'd announced her plans to return to Cedar Springs, her readers had gone wild. They wrote in, offering suggestions as to how she should present her transformed self to her old friends, what she should do for a part-time job, and pretty much everything in between. It never ceased to amaze her how invested her readers were in her life and her weight loss journey. In fact, the whole *returning home* thing had garnered so much attention that a talent agent, Jade Johnson, had contacted Gwen about representation, a book deal, and a possible television deal. It was all too crazy to comprehend, but Gwen wasn't about to say no.

She swallowed the rest of her water quickly. "The next one needs alcohol."

"Really?"

Gwen nodded. "Yes. There are only sixty-four calories in vodka. And I'll just run a few extra miles tomorrow. It'll be worth it."

Deanna laughed. "Sounds good. Well, not the running part. I'll leave that up to you. But I don't have any patients tomorrow, so I'll have a few drinks to toast your return. I'll get Marcus to meet us at the Grizzly Paw when he's done up at the hill. He'll want to meet you. I have trouble remembering that you never knew him."

"Nope." Gwen shook her head. "He moved here after my last summer. But it sounds like a good plan to me." Gwen leaned down to retrieve her laptop from the bag at her feet. "But first I need to post an entry."

"Seriously? You just got here."

"I know." She smiled and tried not to take offense to her friend's expression. Ever since her blog started to get real attention and had actually started to make her money, most people had the same reaction. She'd definitely discovered that people struggled with the idea that you could actually make a living writing about your life. Hell, when the advertising offers had first started coming in, Gwen had trouble believing anyone would actually want to give her money to tell her story. "But it pays the bills, Dee. So as long as people want to read it, I'm going to write it."

She flipped open her laptop, signed onto Deanna's Wi-Fi and logged into her account before her fingers froze over the keys. "What do you think?" she asked her friend. "How should I write about Ian?"

"Ian?" Deanna shook her head. "You can't. I mean, you can't use his name or anything."

"Oh my God. Of course not! I don't use anyone's real name. I don't even say what town I'm in. That part is all anonymous. It has to be. But part of the success of everything is how real it all is. So..."

"You're going to blog about Ian?"

Gwen nodded. There really wasn't a question about it. In fact, she'd already kind of alluded to him in past posts as one of her catalysts for starting her weight loss journey. There was no doubt in her mind that if she'd been thin all those years ago, Ian would never have stood her up at the Summer Equinox festival. Not a chance.

"Wait." Deanna got that look in her eye that meant she'd just figured out the connection. "You've already blogged about him, haven't you?"

"You read my blog?"

Deanna gave her a look. "Of course I do. Since the beginning. And that's when you mentioned...Ian is Mr. Summer. How did I not see that until right now?"

Gwen laughed. "I have no idea. It's not like my feelings for him were a big secret or anything. Doesn't everyone remember my public humiliation?"

Deanna grabbed her hand and squeezed. "Gwen, no one remembers that. I promise."

"I remember."

Her friend laughed a little and moved away. "You're the

only one. It wasn't even a big deal. He just didn't show up. It's not important. Let it go."

But as Deanna moved about the kitchen, cleaning up dishes and leaving Gwen to write her blog post, all she could think of was that it *was* important and there was no way she could let it go.

Dear Reader,

Sometimes things don't turn out quite the way you plan...

If you're anything like me, you've spent some time thinking about and maybe even daydreaming about how certain people from your past will react to seeing the new and healthier version of you after wronging you. Not to say that I've spent a lot of time thinking on this, but I'd be lying if I said I never thought of it. Of course, as I was planning my return to the town I'd spent all my summers, there was one person in particular that came to mind. Mr. Summer. Long-time readers will remember me mentioning Mr. Summer before. Every young woman—particularly those of us who've struggled with our body image...who hasn't—has at least one encounter with a boy or man that has stuck with them. An encounter for better or worse that somehow shaped or defined how they thought of members of the opposite sex, and sadly, how they thought of themselves.

That was Mr. Summer. I was desperately in love with him from the summers of fourteen to eighteen. Four years of my life in which he barely knew I was alive. When he finally did notice me, he humiliated me and broke my heart.

For years, he was the star of my fantasies when I thought about returning with my new and improved self. How would he react? Would his jaw drop? Would he stumble over his words as he apologized for standing me up all those years ago? Would he beg me to give him another chance?

Well, readers, I can tell you that now, all these years later I finally have my answer.

None of those things happened. In fact, he didn't even recognize me. We came eye to eye and there wasn't even a flicker of acknowledgment in his eyes. (Which are still as dreamy as I remember.)

And now I'm here, on the eve of my first night back in town and already I'm filled with a strong sense of dissatisfaction in regards to Mr. Summer. So, obviously I cannot let a homecoming come and go without doing something about it. Or can I?

What do you think? Should I confront Mr. Summer and thank him for being at least one of the catalysts that spurred my life change? Or should I let it go and move on? Or maybe something different....

Read the rest of Love in the Moment NOW and fall in love with the rest of the McCormick brothers!